DOVER · THRIFT · EDITIONS

Macbeth

WILLIAM SHAKESPEARE

DOVER PUBLICATIONS, INC.
New York

DOVER THRIFT EDITIONS
GENERAL EDITOR: STANLEY APPELBAUM
EDITOR OF THIS VOLUME: SHANE WELLER

Performance

This Dover Thrift Edition may be used in its entirety, in adaptation or in any other way for theatrical productions, professional and amateur, in the United States, without fee, permission or acknowledgment. (This may not apply outside of the United States, as copyright conditions may vary.)

Copyright

Bibliographical Note

This Dover edition, first published in 1993, contains the unabridged text of *Macbeth* as published in Volume VII of the second edition of *The Works of William Shakespeare*, Macmillan and Co., London, 1892. The Note and explanatory footnotes were prepared specially for the present edition.

Library of Congress Cataloging-in-Publication Data

Shakespeare, William, 1564–1616.
Macbeth / William Shakespeare.
p. cm. — (Dover Thrift editions)
"This Dover edition, first published in 1993, contains the unabridged text of Macbeth as published in Volume VII of the second edition of The Works of William Shakespeare, Macmillan and Co., London, 1892"—CIP galley.
ISBN 0-486-27802-6 (pbk.)
1. Macbeth, King of Scotland, 11th cent.—Drama. I. Title. II. Series.
PR2823.A1 1993
822.3'3—dc20 93-21799
CIP

Manufactured in the United States of America
Dover Publications, Inc., 31 East 2nd Street, Mineola, N.Y. 11501

Note

In *Macbeth*, the story of a catastrophic regicide, William Shakespeare (1564–1616) offers his most harrowing depiction of evil and the guilt and madness to which it can give rise. Thought to have been written between 1603 and 1606 (after both *Hamlet* and *Othello*), *Macbeth* was most probably first performed in 1606, at Hampton Court, in the presence of King James I (who was reputed to be a descendant of Banquo, one of the victims of Macbeth, an eleventh-century Scottish king). The play is considerably shorter than any of the other great tragedies of Shakespeare's middle period, and the text as it now exists is possibly a truncated and somewhat revised version (with interpolations by other hands) of a lost version. Shakespeare's principal source was Raphael Holinshed's *Chronicles of Scotland*, although there are also numerous allusions to contemporary historical events, most significantly to the notorious Gunpowder Plot of 1605 and the trials that followed the plot's discovery.

The text reprinted here is that of the "Cambridge Shakespeare"; the explanatory footnotes are based on the glosses given in the third edition of Alexander Schmidt's *Shakespeare-Lexicon*.

Contents

Dramatis Personæ

DUNCAN, king of Scotland
MALCOLM, DONALBAIN, } his sons.
MACBETH, BANQUO, } generals of the King's army.
MACDUFF, LENNOX, ROSS, MENTEITH, ANGUS, CAITHNESS, } noblemen of Scotland.
FLEANCE, son to Banquo.
SIWARD, Earl of Northumberland, general of the English forces.
YOUNG SIWARD, his son.
SEYTON, an officer attending on Macbeth.
BOY, son to Macduff.
An English Doctor.
A Scotch Doctor.
A Sergeant.
A Porter.
An Old Man.

Lady MACBETH.
Lady MACDUFF.
Gentlewoman attending on Lady Macbeth.

HECATE.
Three Witches.
Apparitions.

Lords, Gentlemen, Officers, Soldiers, Murderers, Attendants, and Messengers.

SCENE: *Scotland; England.*

Macbeth

WILLIAM SHAKESPEARE

ACT I.

SCENE I. *A desert place.*

Thunder and lightning. Enter three Witches.

FIRST WITCH. When shall we three meet again
In thunder, lightning, or in rain?
SEC. WITCH. When the hurlyburly's done,
When the battle's lost and won.
THIRD WITCH. That will be ere the set of sun.
FIRST WITCH. Where the place?
SEC. WITCH. Upon the heath.
THIRD WITCH. There to meet with Macbeth.
FIRST WITCH. I come, Graymalkin.[1]
ALL. Paddock[2] calls:—anon!
Fair is foul, and foul is fair.
Hover through the fog and filthy air. [*Exeunt.*

SCENE II. *A camp near Forres.*

Alarum within. Enter DUNCAN, MALCOLM, DONALBAIN, LENNOX, *with* Attendants, *meeting a bleeding* Sergeant.

DUN. What bloody man is that? He can report,
As seemeth by his plight, of the revolt
The newest state.

[1] *Graymalkin*] a witches' familiar in the shape of a cat.
[2] *Paddock*] a toad (another witches' familiar).

MAL. This is the sergeant
Who like a good and hardy soldier fought
'Gainst my captivity. Hail, brave friend!
Say to the king the knowledge of the broil
As thou didst leave it.
SER. Doubtful it stood;
As two spent swimmers, that do cling together
And choke their art. The merciless Macdonwald—
Worthy to be a rebel, for to that
The multiplying villanies of nature
Do swarm upon him—from the western isles
Of kerns and gallowglasses[1] is supplied;
And fortune, on his damned quarrel smiling,
Show'd like a rebel's whore: but all's too weak:
For brave Macbeth—well he deserves that name—
Disdaining fortune, with his brandish'd steel,
Which smoked with bloody execution,
Like valour's minion carved out his passage
Till he faced the slave;
Which ne'er shook hands, nor bade farewell to him,
Till he unseam'd him from the nave to the chaps,[2]
And fix'd his head upon our battlements.
DUN. O valiant cousin! worthy gentleman!
SER. As whence the sun 'gins his reflection
Shipwrecking storms and direful thunders break,
So from that spring whence comfort seem'd to come
Discomfort swells. Mark, king of Scotland, mark:
No sooner justice had, with valour arm'd,
Compell'd these skipping kerns to trust their heels,
But the Norweyan lord, surveying vantage,[3]
With furbish'd arms and new supplies of men,
Began a fresh assault.
DUN. Dismay'd not this
Our captains, Macbeth and Banquo?
SER. Yes;
As sparrows eagles, or the hare the lion.

[1] *kerns and gallowglasses*] Irish foot soldiers.
[2] *nave to the chaps*] navel to the jaw.
[3] *surveying vantage*] seeing his opportunity.

If I say sooth, I must report they were
As cannons overcharged with double cracks;
So they
Doubly redoubled strokes upon the foe:
Except they meant to bathe in reeking wounds,
Or memorize another Golgotha,[4]
I cannot tell—
But I am faint; my gashes cry for help.

DUN. So well thy words become thee as thy wounds;
They smack of honour both. Go get him surgeons.
[*Exit Sergeant, attended.*
Who comes here?

Enter ROSS.

MAL. The worthy thane of Ross.

LEN. What a haste looks through his eyes! So should he look
That seems to speak things strange.

ROSS. God save the king!

DUN. Whence camest thou, worthy thane?

ROSS. From Fife, great king;
Where the Norweyan banners flout the sky
And fan our people cold.
Norway himself, with terrible numbers,
Assisted by that most disloyal traitor
The thane of Cawdor, began a dismal[5] conflict;
Till that Bellona's[6] bridegroom, lapp'd in proof,[7]
Confronted him with self-comparisons,[8]
Point against point rebellious, arm 'gainst arm,
Curbing his lavish spirit: and, to conclude,
The victory fell on us.

DUN. Great happiness!

ROSS. That now
Sweno, the Norways' king, craves composition;[9]

[4] *Golgotha*] the place of execution outside Jerusalem; also known as Calvary.
[5] *dismal*] fatal.
[6] *Bellona*] goddess of war.
[7] *lapp'd in proof*] clad in impenetrable armor.
[8] *self-comparisons*] equal force and skill.
[9] *composition*] accord, peace.

Nor would we deign him burial of his men
Till he disbursed, at Saint Colme's inch,[10]
Ten thousand dollars to our general use.

DUN. No more that thane of Cawdor shall deceive
Our bosom interest: go pronounce his present death,
And with his former title greet Macbeth.

ROSS. I'll see it done.

DUN. What he hath lost, noble Macbeth hath won. [*Exeunt.*

SCENE III. *A heath.*

Thunder. Enter the three Witches.

FIRST WITCH. Where hast thou been, sister?

SEC. WITCH. Killing swine.

THIRD WITCH. Sister, where thou?

FIRST WITCH. A sailor's wife had chestnuts in her lap,
And mounch'd,[1] and mounch'd, and mounch'd. 'Give me,' quoth I:
'Aroint thee,[2] witch!' the rump-fed ronyon[3] cries.
Her husband's to Aleppo gone, master o' the Tiger:
But in a sieve I'll thither sail,
And, like a rat without a tail,
I'll do, I'll do, and I'll do.

SEC. WITCH. I'll give thee a wind.

FIRST WITCH. Thou'rt kind.

THIRD WITCH. And I another.

FIRST WITCH. I myself have all the other;
And the very ports they blow,
All the quarters that they know
I' the shipman's card.[4]
I will drain him dry as hay:

[10] *inch*] island.
[1] *mounch'd*] munched.
[2] *Aroint thee*] begone.
[3] *ronyon*] mangy creature.
[4] *shipman's card*] compass or chart.

Sleep shall neither night nor day
Hang upon his pent-house lid;[5]
He shall live a man forbid:
Weary se'nnights nine times nine
Shall he dwindle, peak,[6] and pine:
Though his bark cannot be lost,
Yet it shall be tempest-tost.
Look what I have.

SEC. WITCH. Show me, show me.

FIRST WITCH. Here I have a pilot's thumb,
Wreck'd as homeward he did come. [*Drum within.*

THIRD WITCH. A drum, a drum!
Macbeth doth come.

ALL. The weird sisters, hand in hand,
Posters[7] of the sea and land,
Thus do go about, about:
Thrice to thine, and thrice to mine,
And thrice again, to make up nine.
Peace! the charm's wound up.

Enter MACBETH *and* BANQUO.

MACB. So foul and fair a day I have not seen.

BAN. How far is't call'd to Forres? What are these
So wither'd, and so wild in their attire,
That look not like the inhabitants o' the earth,
And yet are on't? Live you? or are you aught
That man may question? You seem to understand me,
By each at once her choppy[8] finger laying
Upon her skinny lips: you should be women,
And yet your beards forbid me to interpret
That you are so.

MACB. Speak, if you can: what are you?

FIRST WITCH. All hail, Macbeth! hail to thee, thane of Glamis!

SEC. WITCH. All hail, Macbeth! hail to thee, thane of Cawdor!

[5] *pent-house lid*] eyelid.
[6] *peak*] grow thin.
[7] *Posters*] swift travelers.
[8] *choppy*] chapped.

THIRD WITCH. All hail, Macbeth, that shalt be king hereafter!
BAN. Good sir, why do you start, and seem to fear
Things that do sound so fair? I' the name of truth,
Are ye fantastical,[9] or that indeed
Which outwardly ye show? My noble partner
You greet with present grace and great prediction
Of noble having[10] and of royal hope,
That he seems rapt withal: to me you speak not:
If you can look into the seeds of time,
And say which grain will grow and which will not,
Speak then to me, who neither beg nor fear
Your favours nor your hate.
FIRST WITCH. Hail!
SEC. WITCH. Hail!
THIRD WITCH. Hail!
FIRST WITCH. Lesser than Macbeth, and greater.
SEC. WITCH. Not so happy, yet much happier.
THIRD WITCH. Thou shalt get kings, though thou be none:
So all hail, Macbeth and Banquo!
FIRST WITCH. Banquo and Macbeth, all hail!
MACB. Stay, you imperfect speakers, tell me more:
By Sinel's death I know I am thane of Glamis;
But how of Cawdor? the thane of Cawdor lives,
A prosperous gentleman; and to be king
Stands not within the prospect of belief,
No more than to be Cawdor. Say from whence
You owe[11] this strange intelligence? or why
Upon this blasted heath you stop our way
With such prophetic greeting? Speak, I charge you.
[*Witches vanish*.
BAN. The earth hath bubbles as the water has,
And these are of them: whither are they vanish'd?
MACB. Into the air, and what seem'd corporal melted
As breath into the wind. Would they had stay'd!
BAN. Were such things here as we do speak about?

[9] *fantastical*] imaginary.
[10] *having*] estate, property.
[11] *owe*] possess.

Or have we eaten on the insane root
That takes the reason prisoner?

MACB. Your children shall be kings.

BAN. You shall be king.

MACB. And thane of Cawdor too: went it not so?

BAN. To the selfsame tune and words. Who's here?

Enter ROSS *and* ANGUS.

ROSS. The king hath happily received, Macbeth,
The news of thy success: and when he reads
Thy personal venture in the rebels' fight,
His wonders and his praises do contend
Which should be thine or his: silenced with that,
In viewing o'er the rest o' the selfsame day,
He finds thee in the stout Norweyan ranks,
Nothing afeard of what thyself didst make,
Strange images of death. As thick as hail
Came post with post, and every one did bear
Thy praises in his kingdom's great defence,
And pour'd them down before him.

ANG. We are sent
To give thee, from our royal master, thanks;
Only to herald thee into his sight,
Not pay thee.

ROSS. And for an earnest[12] of a greater honour,
He bade me, from him, call thee thane of Cawdor:
In which addition,[13] hail, most worthy thane!
For it is thine.

BAN. What, can the devil speak true?

MACB. The thane of Cawdor lives: why do you dress me
In borrow'd robes?

ANG. Who was the thane lives yet,
But under heavy judgement bears that life
Which he deserves to lose. Whether he was combined
With those of Norway, or did line[14] the rebel
With hidden help and vantage, or that with both

[12] *earnest*] portion paid as a pledge.
[13] *addition*] title.
[14] *line*] strengthen.

He labour'd in his country's wreck, I know not;
But treasons capital, confess'd and proved,
Have overthrown him.

MACB. [*Aside*] Glamis, and thane of Cawdor:
The greatest is behind.—Thanks for your pains.—
Do you not hope your children shall be kings,
When those that gave the thane of Cawdor to me
Promised no less to them?

BAN. That, trusted home,
Might yet enkindle you unto the crown,
Besides the thane of Cawdor. But 'tis strange:
And oftentimes, to win us to our harm,
The instruments of darkness tell us truths,
Win us with honest trifles, to betray's
In deepest consequence.
Cousins, a word, I pray you.

MACB. [*Aside*] Two truths are told,
As happy prologues to the swelling act
Of the imperial theme.—I thank you, gentlemen.—
[*Aside*] This supernatural soliciting
Cannot be ill; cannot be good: if ill,
Why hath it given me earnest of success,
Commencing in a truth? I am thane of Cawdor:
If good, why do I yield to that suggestion
Whose horrid image doth unfix my hair
And make my seated heart knock at my ribs,
Against the use of nature? Present fears
Are less than horrible imaginings:
My thought, whose murder yet is but fantastical,
Shakes so my single state of man that function
Is smother'd in surmise, and nothing is
But what is not.

BAN. Look, how our partner's rapt.

MACB. [*Aside*] If chance will have me king, why, chance may crown me,
Without my stir.

BAN. New honours come upon him,
Like our strange garments, cleave not to their mould
But with the aid of use.

MACB. [*Aside*] Come what come may,

Time and the hour runs through the roughest day.
BAN. Worthy Macbeth, we stay upon your leisure.
MACB. Give me your favour:[15] my dull brain was wrought
With things forgotten. Kind gentlemen, your pains
Are register'd where every day I turn
The leaf to read them. Let us toward the king.
Think upon what hath chanced, and at more time,
The interim having weigh'd it, let us speak
Our free hearts each to other.
BAN. Very gladly.
MACB. Till then, enough. Come, friends. [*Exeunt.*

SCENE IV. *Forres. The palace.*

Flourish. Enter DUNCAN, MALCOLM, DONALBAIN, LENNOX, *and* Attendants.

DUN. Is execution done on Cawdor? Are not
Those in commission yet return'd?
MAL. My liege,
They are not yet come back. But I have spoke
With one that saw him die, who did report
That very frankly he confess'd his treasons,
Implored your highness' pardon and set forth
A deep repentance: nothing in his life
Became him like the leaving it; he died
As one that had been studied in his death,
To throw away the dearest thing he owed
As 'twere a careless trifle.
DUN. There's no art
To find the mind's construction in the face:
He was a gentleman on whom I built
An absolute trust.

[15] *favour*] pardon.

Enter MACBETH, BANQUO, ROSS, *and* ANGUS.

O worthiest cousin!
The sin of my ingratitude even now
Was heavy on me: thou art so far before,
That swiftest wing of recompense is slow
To overtake thee. Would thou hadst less deserved,
That the proportion both of thanks and payment
Might have been mine! only I have left to say,
More is thy due than more than all can pay.

MACB. The service and the loyalty I owe,
In doing it, pays itself. Your highness' part
Is to receive our duties: and our duties
Are to your throne and state children and servants;
Which do but what they should, by doing every thing
Safe toward[1] your love and honour.

DUN. Welcome hither:
I have begun to plant thee, and will labour
To make thee full of growing. Noble Banquo,
That hast no less deserved, nor must be known
No less to have done so: let me infold thee
And hold thee to my heart.

BAN. There if I grow,
The harvest is your own.

DUN. My plenteous joys,
Wanton in fulness, seek to hide themselves
In drops of sorrow. Sons, kinsmen, thanes,
And you whose places are the nearest, know,
We will establish our estate upon
Our eldest, Malcolm, whom we name hereafter
The Prince of Cumberland: which honour must
Not unaccompanied invest him only,
But signs of nobleness, like stars, shall shine
On all deservers. From hence to Inverness,
And bind us further to you.

MACB. The rest is labour, which is not used for you:
I'll be myself the harbinger, and make joyful
The hearing of my wife with your approach;

[1] *Safe toward*] to secure (or consistent with).

So humbly take my leave.
DUN. My worthy Cawdor!
MACB. [*Aside*] The Prince of Cumberland! that is a step
On which I must fall down, or else o'erleap,
For in my way it lies. Stars, hide your fires;
Let not light see my black and deep desires:
The eye wink at the hand; yet let that be
Which the eye fears, when it is done, to see. [*Exit.*
DUN. True, worthy Banquo; he is full so valiant,
And in his commendations I am fed;
It is a banquet to me. Let's after him,
Whose care is gone before to bid us welcome:
It is a peerless kinsman. [*Flourish. Exeunt.*

SCENE V. *Inverness. Macbeth's castle.*

Enter LADY MACBETH, *reading a letter.*

LADY M. 'They met me in the day of success; and I have learned by the perfectest report, they have more in them than mortal knowledge. When I burned in desire to question them further, they made themselves air, into which they vanished. Whiles I stood rapt in the wonder of it, came missives[1] from the king, who all-hailed me "Thane of Cawdor"; by which title, before, these weird sisters saluted me, and referred me to the coming on of time, with "Hail, king that shalt be!" This have I thought good to deliver thee, my dearest partner of greatness, that thou mightst not lose the dues of rejoicing, by being ignorant of what greatness is promised thee. Lay it to thy heart, and farewell.'

Glamis thou art, and Cawdor, and shalt be
What thou art promised: yet do I fear thy nature;
It is too full o' the milk of human kindness
To catch the nearest way: thou wouldst be great;
Art not without ambition, but without

[1] *missives*] messengers.

The illness[2] should attend it: what thou wouldst highly,
That wouldst thou holily; wouldst not play false,
And yet wouldst wrongly win: thou 'ldst have, great Glamis,
That which cries 'Thus thou must do, if thou have it;
And that which rather thou dost fear to do
Than wishest should be undone.' Hie thee hither,
That I may pour my spirits in thine ear,
And chastise with the valour of my tongue
All that impedes thee from the golden round,
Which fate and metaphysical[3] aid doth seem
To have thee crown'd withal.

Enter a MESSENGER.

What is your tidings?

MESS. The king comes here to-night.

LADY M. Thou'rt mad to say it:
Is not thy master with him? who, were't so,
Would have inform'd for preparation.

MESS. So please you, it is true: our thane is coming:
One of my fellows had the speed of him,
Who, almost dead for breath, had scarcely more
Than would make up his message.

LADY M. Give him tending;
He brings great news. [*Exit Messenger.*
The raven himself is hoarse
That croaks the fatal entrance of Duncan
Under my battlements. Come, you spirits
That tend on mortal[4] thoughts, unsex me here,
And fill me, from the crown to the toe, top-full
Of direst cruelty! make thick my blood,
Stop up the access and passage to remorse,[5]
That no compunctious visitings of nature
Shake my fell purpose, nor keep peace between
The effect and it! Come to my woman's breasts,

[2] *illness*] wickedness.
[3] *metaphysical*] supernatural.
[4] *mortal*] deadly, murderous.
[5] *remorse*] pity, tenderness.

And take[6] my milk for gall, you murdering ministers,
Wherever in your sightless[7] substances
You wait on nature's mischief! Come, thick night,
And pall thee in the dunnest smoke of hell,
That my keen knife see not the wound it makes,
Nor heaven peep through the blanket of the dark,
To cry 'Hold, hold!'

Enter MACBETH.

Great Glamis! worthy Cawdor!
Greater than both, by the all-hail hereafter!
Thy letters have transported me beyond
This ignorant present, and I feel now
The future in the instant.

MACB. My dearest love,
Duncan comes here to-night.

LADY M. And when goes hence?

MACB. To-morrow, as he purposes.

LADY M. O, never
Shall sun that morrow see!
Your face, my thane, is as a book where men
May read strange matters. To beguile the time,[8]
Look like the time; bear welcome in your eye,
Your hand, your tongue: look like the innocent flower,
But be the serpent under't. He that's coming
Must be provided for: and you shall put
This night's great business into my dispatch;
Which shall to all our nights and days to come
Give solely sovereign sway and masterdom.

MACB. We will speak further.

LADY M. Only look up clear;
To alter favour[9] ever is to fear:
Leave all the rest to me. [*Exeunt*.

[6] *take*] exchange.
[7] *sightless*] invisible.
[8] *time*] world, others.
[9] *favour*] expression, countenance.

SCENE VI. *Before Macbeth's castle.*

Hautboys and torches. Enter DUNCAN, MALCOLM, DONALBAIN, BANQUO, LENNOX, MACDUFF, ROSS, ANGUS, *and* Attendants.

DUN. This castle hath a pleasant seat; the air
Nimbly and sweetly recommends itself
Unto our gentle senses.

BAN. This guest of summer,
The temple-haunting martlet,[1] does approve[2]
By his loved mansionry that the heaven's breath
Smells wooingly here: no jutty,[3] frieze,
Buttress, nor coign[4] of vantage, but this bird
Hath made his pendent bed and procreant cradle:
Where they most breed and haunt, I have observed
The air is delicate.

Enter LADY MACBETH.

DUN. See, see, our honour'd hostess!
The love that follows us sometime is our trouble,
Which still we thank as love. Herein I teach you
How you shall bid God 'ild[5] us for your pains,
And thank us for your trouble.

LADY M. All our service
In every point twice done, and then done double,
Were poor and single business to contend
Against those honours deep and broad wherewith
Your majesty loads our house: for those of old,
And the late dignities heap'd up to them,
We rest your hermits.[6]

DUN. Where's the thane of Cawdor?
We coursed him at the heels, and had a purpose

[1] *martlet*] house-martin.
[2] *approve*] prove.
[3] *jutty*] projection.
[4] *coign*] corner.
[5] *'ild*] reward.
[6] *hermits*] beadsmen, those who pray for another.

To be his purveyor:[7] but he rides well,
And his great love, sharp as his spur, hath holp him
To his home before us. Fair and noble hostess,
We are your guest to-night.

LADY M. Your servants ever
Have theirs, themselves, and what is theirs, in compt,[8]
To make their audit at your highness' pleasure,
Still to return your own.

DUN. Give me your hand;
Conduct me to mine host: we love him highly,
And shall continue our graces towards him.
By your leave, hostess. [*Exeunt.*

SCENE VII. *Macbeth's castle.*

Hautboys and torches. Enter a Sewer,[1] *and divers* Servants *with dishes and service, and pass over the stage. Then enter* MACBETH.

MACB. If it were done when 'tis done, then 'twere well
It were done quickly: if the assassination
Could trammel up[2] the consequence, and catch,
With his surcease,[3] success; that but this blow
Might be the be-all and the end-all here,
But here, upon this bank and shoal of time,
We'ld jump the life to come. But in these cases
We still have judgement here; that we but teach
Bloody instructions, which being taught return
To plague the inventor: this even-handed justice
Commends the ingredients of our poison'd chalice
To our own lips. He's here in double trust:
First, as I am his kinsman and his subject,

[7] *purveyor*] provider.
[8] *compt*] account.

[1] *Sewer*] head servant.
[2] *trammel up*] tie up or catch in a net.
[3] *surcease*] death.

Strong both against the deed; then, as his host,
Who should against his murderer shut the door,
Not bear the knife myself. Besides, this Duncan
Hath borne his faculties[4] so meek, hath been
So clear[5] in his great office, that his virtues
Will plead like angels trumpet-tongued against
The deep damnation of his taking-off;
And pity, like a naked new-born babe,
Striding[6] the blast, or heaven's cherubin horsed
Upon the sightless couriers of the air,
Shall blow the horrid deed in every eye,
That tears shall drown the wind. I have no spur
To prick the sides of my intent, but only
Vaulting ambition, which o'erleaps itself
And falls on the other.[7]

Enter LADY MACBETH.

How now! what news?

LADY M. He has almost supp'd: why have you left the chamber?
MACB. Hath he ask'd for me?
LADY M. Know you not he has?
MACB. We will proceed no further in this business:
He hath honour'd me of late; and I have bought
Golden opinions from all sorts of people,
Which would be worn now in their newest gloss,
Not cast aside so soon.
LADY M. Was the hope drunk
Wherein you dress'd yourself? hath it slept since?
And wakes it now, to look so green and pale
At what it did so freely? From this time
Such I account thy love. Art thou afeard
To be the same in thine own act and valour
As thou art in desire? Wouldst thou have that
Which thou esteem'st the ornament of life,
And live a coward in thine own esteem,

[4] *faculties*] powers.
[5] *clear*] irreproachable.
[6] *Striding*] bestriding, mounting.
[7] *other*] other side (of the horse).

Letting 'I dare not' wait upon 'I would,'
Like the poor cat i' the adage?

MACB. Prithee, peace:
I dare do all that may become a man;
Who dares do more is none.

LADY M. What beast was't then
That made you break this enterprise to me?
When you durst do it, then you were a man;
And, to be more than what you were, you would
Be so much more the man. Nor time nor place
Did then adhere, and yet you would make both:
They have made themselves, and that their fitness now
Does unmake you. I have given suck, and know
How tender 'tis to love the babe that milks me:
I would, while it was smiling in my face,
Have pluck'd my nipple from his boneless gums,
And dash'd the brains out, had I so sworn as you
Have done to this.

MACB. If we should fail?

LADY M. We fail!
But screw your courage to the sticking-place,
And we'll not fail. When Duncan is asleep—
Whereto the rather shall his day's hard journey
Soundly invite him—his two chamberlains
Will I with wine and wassail so convince,[8]
That memory, the warder of the brain,
Shall be a fume, and the receipt of reason
A limbec[9] only: when in swinish sleep
Their drenched natures lie as in a death,
What cannot you and I perform upon
The unguarded Duncan? what not put upon
His spongy officers, who shall bear the guilt
Of our great quell?[10]

MACB. Bring forth men-children only;
For thy undaunted mettle should compose
Nothing but males. Will it not be received,

[8] *convince*] overcome.
[9] *limbec*] alembic, still.
[10] *quell*] murder.

When we have mark'd with blood those sleepy two
Of his own chamber, and used their very daggers,
That they have done't?

LADY M. Who dares receive it other,
As we shall make our griefs and clamour roar
Upon his death?

MACB. I am settled, and bend up
Each corporal agent to this terrible feat.
Away, and mock the time with fairest show:
False face must hide what the false heart doth know. [*Exeunt.*

ACT II.

SCENE I. *Inverness. Court of Macbeth's castle.*

Enter BANQUO, *and* FLEANCE *bearing a torch before him.*

BAN. How goes the night, boy?
FLE. The moon is down; I have not heard the clock.
BAN. And she goes down at twelve.
FLE. I take't, 'tis later, sir.
BAN. Hold, take my sword. There's husbandry in heaven,
Their candles are all out. Take thee that too.
A heavy summons lies like lead upon me,
And yet I would not sleep. Merciful powers,
Restrain in me the cursed thoughts that nature
Gives way to in repose!

Enter MACBETH, *and a* Servant *with a torch.*

Give me my sword.
Who's there?
MACB. A friend.
BAN. What, sir, not yet at rest? The king's a-bed:
He hath been in unusual pleasure, and
Sent forth great largess to your offices:[1]
This diamond he greets your wife withal,
By the name of most kind hostess; and shut up
In measureless content.
MACB. Being unprepared,
Our will became the servant to defect,
Which else should free have wrought.
BAN. All's well.

[1] *offices*] servants' quarters.

I dreamt last night of the three weird sisters:
To you they have show'd some truth.

MACB. I think not of them:
Yet, when we can entreat an hour to serve,
We would spend it in some words upon that business,
If you would grant the time.

BAN. At your kind'st leisure.

MACB. If you shall cleave to my consent, when 'tis,
It shall make honour for you.

BAN. So I lose none
In seeking to augment it, but still keep
My bosom franchised and allegiance clear,
I shall be counsell'd.

MACB. Good repose the while!

BAN. Thanks, sir: the like to you! [*Exeunt Banquo and Fleance.*

MACB. Go bid thy mistress, when my drink is ready,
She strike upon the bell. Get thee to bed. [*Exit Servant.*
Is this a dagger which I see before me,
The handle toward my hand? Come, let me clutch thee.
I have thee not, and yet I see thee still.
Art thou not, fatal vision, sensible
To feeling as to sight? or art thou but
A dagger of the mind, a false creation,
Proceeding from the heat-oppressed brain?
I see thee yet, in form as palpable
As this which now I draw.
Thou marshall'st me the way that I was going;
And such an instrument I was to use.
Mine eyes are made the fools o' the other senses,
Or else worth all the rest: I see thee still;
And on thy blade and dudgeon[2] gouts[3] of blood,
Which was not so before. There's no such thing:
It is the bloody business which informs
Thus to mine eyes. Now o'er the one half-world
Nature seems dead, and wicked dreams abuse
The curtain'd sleep; witchcraft celebrates
Pale Hecate's offerings; and wither'd murder,

[2] *dudgeon*] handle.
[3] *gouts*] drops.

Alarum'd by his sentinel, the wolf,
Whose howl's his watch, thus with his stealthy pace,
With Tarquin's ravishing strides, towards his design
Moves like a ghost. Thou sure and firm-set earth,
Hear not my steps, which way they walk, for fear
Thy very stones prate of my whereabout,
And take the present horror from the time,
Which now suits with it. Whiles I threat, he lives:
Words to the heat of deeds too cold breath gives. [A *bell rings*.
I go, and it is done: the bell invites me.
Hear it not, Duncan, for it is a knell
That summons thee to heaven, or to hell. [*Exit*.

SCENE II. *The same.*

Enter LADY MACBETH.

LADY M. That which hath made them drunk hath made me bold;
What hath quench'd them hath given me fire. Hark! Peace!
It was the owl that shriek'd, the fatal bellman,
Which gives the stern'st good-night. He is about it:
The doors are open, and the surfeited grooms[1]
Do mock their charge with snores: I have drugg'd their possets,[2]
That death and nature do contend about them,
Whether they live or die.

MACB. [*Within*] Who's there? what, ho!

LADY M. Alack, I am afraid they have awaked
And 'tis not done: the attempt and not the deed
Confounds us. Hark! I laid their daggers ready;
He could not miss 'em. Had he not resembled
My father as he slept, I had done't.

[1] *grooms*] menials.
[2] *possets*] bedtime drink of hot milk curdled with ale.

Enter MACBETH.

My husband!

MACB. I have done the deed. Didst thou not hear a noise?

LADY M. I heard the owl scream and the crickets cry.
Did not you speak?

MACB. When?

LADY M. Now.

MACB. As I descended?

LADY M. Ay.

MACB. Hark!
Who lies i' the second chamber?

LADY M. Donalbain.

MACB. This is a sorry sight. [*Looking on his hands.*

LADY M. A foolish thought, to say a sorry sight.

MACB. There's one did laugh in's sleep, and one cried 'Murder!'
That they did wake each other: I stood and heard them:
But they did say their prayers, and address'd them[3]
Again to sleep.

LADY M. There are two lodged together.

MACB. One cried 'God bless us!' and 'Amen' the other,
As they had seen me with these hangman's hands:
Listening their fear, I could not say 'Amen,'
When they did say 'God bless us!'

LADY M. Consider it not so deeply.

MACB. But wherefore could not I pronounce 'Amen'?
I had most need of blessing, and 'Amen'
Stuck in my throat.

LADY M. These deeds must not be thought
After these ways; so, it will make us mad.

MACB. Methought I heard a voice cry 'Sleep no more!
Macbeth does murder sleep'—the innocent sleep,
Sleep that knits up the ravell'd sleave[4] of care,
The death of each day's life, sore labour's bath,
Balm of hurt minds, great nature's second course,
Chief nourisher in life's feast,—

[3] *address'd them*] made themselves ready.
[4] *sleave*] silk.

LADY M. What do you mean?
MACB. Still it cried 'Sleep no more!' to all the house:
'Glamis hath murder'd sleep, and therefore Cawdor
Shall sleep no more: Macbeth shall sleep no more.'
LADY M. Who was it that thus cried? Why, worthy thane,
You do unbend your noble strength, to think
So brainsickly of things. Go get some water,
And wash this filthy witness from your hand.
Why did you bring these daggers from the place?
They must lie there: go carry them, and smear
The sleepy grooms with blood.
MACB. I'll go no more:
I am afraid to think what I have done;
Look on't again I dare not.
LADY M. Infirm of purpose!
Give me the daggers: the sleeping and the dead
Are but as pictures: 'tis the eye of childhood
That fears a painted devil. If he do bleed,
I'll gild the faces of the grooms withal,
For it must seem their guilt. [*Exit. Knocking within.*
MACB. Whence is that knocking?
How is't with me, when every noise appals me?
What hands are here? ha! they pluck out mine eyes!
Will all great Neptune's ocean wash this blood
Clean from my hand? No; this my hand will rather
The multitudinous seas incarnadine,
Making the green one red.

Re-enter LADY MACBETH.

LADY M. My hands are of your colour, but I shame
To wear a heart so white. [*Knocking within.*] I hear a knocking
At the south entry: retire we to our chamber:
A little water clears us of this deed:
How easy is it then! Your constancy
Hath left you unattended.[5] [*Knocking within.*] Hark! more knocking:
Get on your nightgown, lest occasion call us
And show us to be watchers: be not lost

[5] *left you unattended*] abandoned you.

So poorly in your thoughts.
MACB. To know my deed, 'twere best not know myself.
[*Knocking within.*
Wake Duncan with thy knocking! I would thou couldst!
[*Exeunt.*

SCENE III. *The same.*

Enter a Porter. *Knocking within.*

PORTER. Here's a knocking indeed! If a man were porter of hell-gate, he should have old[1] turning the key. [*Knocking within.*] Knock, knock, knock! Who's there, i' the name of Beelzebub? Here's a farmer, that hanged himself on th' expectation of plenty:[2] come in time; have napkins enow about you; here you'll sweat for't. [*Knocking within.*] Knock, knock! Who's there, in th' other devil's name? Faith, here's an equivocator, that could swear in both the scales against either scale; who committed treason enough for God's sake, yet could not equivocate to heaven: O, come in, equivocator. [*Knocking within.*] Knock, knock, knock! Who's there? Faith, here's an English tailor come hither, for stealing out of a French hose: come in, tailor; here you may roast your goose.[3] [*Knocking within.*] Knock, knock; never at quiet! What are you? But this place is too cold for hell. I'll devil-porter it no further: I had thought to have let in some of all professions, that go the primrose way to the everlasting bonfire. [*Knocking within.*] Anon, anon! I pray you, remember the porter. [*Opens the gate.*

Enter MACDUFF *and* LENNOX.

MACD. Was it so late, friend, ere you went to bed,
That you do lie so late?

[1] *old*] too much.
[2] *expectation of plenty*] i.e., low prices.
[3] *goose*] smoothing iron.

PORT. Faith, sir, we were carousing till the second cock: and drink, sir, is a great provoker of three things.

MACD. What three things does drink especially provoke?

PORT. Marry, sir, nose-painting, sleep and urine. Lechery, sir, it provokes and unprovokes; it provokes the desire, but it takes away the performance: therefore much drink may be said to be an equivocator with lechery: it makes him and it mars him; it sets him on and it takes him off; it persuades him and disheartens him; makes him stand to and not stand to; in conclusion, equivocates him in a sleep, and giving him the lie, leaves him.

MACD. I believe drink gave thee the lie last night.

PORT. That it did, sir, i' the very throat on me: but I requited him for his lie, and, I think, being too strong for him, though he took up my legs sometime, yet I made a shift[4] to cast him.

MACD. Is thy master stirring?

Enter MACBETH.

Our knocking has awaked him; here he comes.

LEN. Good morrow, noble sir.

MACB. Good morrow, both.

MACD. Is the king stirring, worthy thane?

MACB. Not yet.

MACD. He did command me to call timely on him:
I have almost slipp'd the hour.

MACB. I'll bring you to him.

MACD. I know this is a joyful trouble to you;
But yet 'tis one.

MACB. The labour we delight in physics pain.
This is the door.

MACD. I'll make so bold to call,
For 'tis my limited[5] service. [*Exit*.

LEN. Goes the king hence to-day?

MACB. He does: he did appoint so.

LEN. The night has been unruly: where we lay,
Our chimneys were blown down, and, as they say,
Lamentings heard i' the air, strange screams of death,

[4] *made a shift*] contrived.
[5] *limited*] appointed.

And prophesying with accents terrible
Of dire combustion and confused events
New hatch'd to the woful time: the obscure bird
Clamour'd the livelong night: some say, the earth
Was feverous and did shake.

MACB. 'Twas a rough night.

LEN. My young remembrance cannot parallel
A fellow to it.

Re-enter MACDUFF.

MACD. O horror, horror, horror! Tongue nor heart
Cannot conceive nor name thee.

MACB. }
LEN. } What's the matter?

MACD. Confusion now hath made his masterpiece.
Most sacrilegious murder hath broke ope
The Lord's anointed temple, and stole thence
The life o' the building.

MACB. What is't you say? the life?

LEN. Mean you his majesty?

MACD. Approach the chamber, and destroy your sight
With a new Gorgon: do not bid me speak;
See, and then speak yourselves. [*Exeunt Macbeth and Lennox.*
Awake, awake!
Ring the alarum-bell. Murder and treason!
Banquo and Donalbain! Malcolm! awake!
Shake off this downy sleep, death's counterfeit,
And look on death itself! up, up, and see
The great doom's image! Malcolm! Banquo!
As from your graves rise up, and walk like sprites,
To countenance[6] this horror. Ring the bell. [*Bell rings.*

Enter LADY MACBETH.

LADY M. What's the business,
That such a hideous trumpet calls to parley
The sleepers of the house? speak, speak!

MACD. O gentle lady,

[6] *countenance*] be in keeping with and behold.

'Tis not for you to hear what I can speak:
The repetition, in a woman's ear,
Would murder as it fell.

Enter BANQUO.

O Banquo, Banquo!
Our royal master's murder'd.

LADY M. Woe, alas!
What, in our house?

BAN. Too cruel any where.
Dear Duff, I prithee, contradict thyself,
And say it is not so.

Re-enter MACBETH *and* LENNOX, *with* ROSS.

MACB. Had I but died an hour before this chance,
I had lived a blessed time; for from this instant
There's nothing serious in morality:[7]
All is but toys: renown and grace is dead;
The wine of life is drawn, and the mere lees
Is left this vault to brag of.

Enter MALCOLM *and* DONALBAIN.

DON. What is amiss?

MACB. You are, and do not know't:
The spring, the head, the fountain of your blood
Is stopp'd; the very source of it is stopp'd.

MACD. Your royal father's murder'd.

MAL. O, by whom?

LEN. Those of his chamber, as it seem'd, had done't:
Their hands and faces were all badged with blood;
So were their daggers, which unwiped we found
Upon their pillows:
They stared, and were distracted; no man's life
Was to be trusted with them.

MACB. O, yet I do repent me of my fury,
That I did kill them.

MACD. Wherefore did you so?

[7] *mortality*] human life.

MACB. Who can be wise, amazed, temperate and furious,
Loyal and neutral, in a moment? No man:
The expedition of my violent love
Outrun the pauser reason. Here lay Duncan,
His silver skin laced with his golden blood,
And his gash'd stabs look'd like a breach in nature
For ruin's wasteful[8] entrance: there, the murderers,
Steep'd in the colours of their trade, their daggers
Unmannerly breech'd[9] with gore: who could refrain,
That had a heart to love, and in that heart
Courage to make's love known?

LADY M. Help me hence, ho!

MACD. Look to the lady.

MAL. [*Aside to Don.*] Why do we hold our tongues,
That most may claim this argument for ours?

DON. [*Aside to Mal.*] What should be spoken here, where our fate,
Hid in an auger-hole, may rush, and seize us?
Let's away;
Our tears are not yet brew'd.

MAL. [*Aside to Don.*] Nor our strong sorrow
Upon the foot of motion.

BAN. Look to the lady:
[*Lady Macbeth is carried out.*
And when we have our naked frailties hid,
That suffer in exposure, let us meet,
And question this most bloody piece of work,
To know it further. Fears and scruples[10] shake us:
In the great hand of God I stand, and thence
Against the undivulged pretence[11] I fight
Of treasonous malice.

MACD. And so do I.

ALL. So all.

MACB. Let's briefly put on manly readiness,
And meet i' the hall together.

[8] *wasteful*] destructive.
[9] *breech'd*] sheathed, covered.
[10] *scruples*] doubts.
[11] *pretence*] purpose, design.

ALL. Well contented.

[*Exeunt all but Malcolm and Donalbain.*

MAL. What will you do? Let's not consort with them:
To show an unfelt sorrow is an office
Which the false man does easy. I'll to England.
DON. To Ireland, I; our separated fortune
Shall keep us both the safer: where we are
There's daggers in men's smiles: the near in blood,
The nearer bloody.
MAL. This murderous shaft that's shot
Hath not yet lighted, and our safest way
Is to avoid the aim. Therefore to horse;
And let us not be dainty of leave-taking,
But shift away:[12] there's warrant in that theft
Which steals itself when there's no mercy left. [*Exeunt.*

SCENE IV. *Outside Macbeth's castle.*

Enter ROSS *with an* old Man.

OLD M. Threescore and ten I can remember well:
Within the volume of which time I have seen
Hours dreadful and things strange, but this sore night
Hath trifled former knowings.
ROSS. Ah, good father,
Thou seest, the heavens, as troubled with man's act,
Threaten his bloody stage: by the clock 'tis day,
And yet dark night strangles the travelling lamp:
Is't night's predominance, or the day's shame,
That darkness does the face of earth entomb,
When living light should kiss it?
OLD M. 'Tis unnatural,

[12] *shift away*] contrive to get away.

Even like the deed that's done. On Tuesday last
A falcon towering in her pride of place
Was by a mousing owl hawk'd at and kill'd.

ROSS. And Duncan's horses—a thing most strange and certain—
Beauteous and swift, the minions[1] of their race,
Turn'd wild in nature, broke their stalls, flung out,
Contending 'gainst obedience, as they would make
War with mankind.

OLD M. 'Tis said they eat each other.

ROSS. They did so, to the amazement of mine eyes,
That look'd upon't.

Enter MACDUFF.

Here comes the good Macduff.
How goes the world, sir, now?

MACD. Why, see you not?

ROSS. Is't known who did this more than bloody deed?

MACD. Those that Macbeth hath slain.

ROSS. Alas, the day!
What good could they pretend?[2]

MACD. They were suborn'd:
Malcolm and Donalbain, the king's two sons,
Are stol'n away and fled, which puts upon them
Suspicion of the deed.

ROSS. 'Gainst nature still:
Thriftless ambition, that wilt ravin up
Thine own life's means! Then 'tis most like
The sovereignty will fall upon Macbeth.

MACD. He is already named, and gone to Scone
To be invested.

ROSS. Where is Duncan's body?

MACD. Carried to Colme-kill,
The sacred storehouse of his predecessors
And guardian of their bones.

ROSS. Will you to Scone?

MACD. No, cousin, I'll to Fife.

[1] *minions*] darlings, favorites.
[2] *pretend*] intend.

ROSS. Well, I will thither.
MACD. Well, may you see things well done there: adieu!
Lest our old robes sit easier than our new!
ROSS. Farewell, father.
OLD M. God's benison go with you, and with those
That would make good of bad and friends of foes! [*Exeunt*.

ACT III.

SCENE I. *Forres. The palace.*

Enter BANQUO.

BAN. Thou hast it now: king, Cawdor, Glamis, all,
As the weird women promised, and I fear
Thou play'dst most foully for't: yet it was said
It should not stand in thy posterity,
But that myself should be the root and father
Of many kings. If there come truth from them—
As upon thee, Macbeth, their speeches shine—
Why, by the verities on thee made good,
May they not be my oracles as well
And set me up in hope? But hush, no more.

Sennet sounded. Enter MACBETH, *as king;* LADY MACBETH, *as queen;* LENNOX, ROSS, Lords, Ladies, *and* Attendants.

MACB. Here's our chief guest.
LADY M. If he had been forgotten,
It had been as a gap in our great feast,
And all-thing[1] unbecoming.
MACB. To-night we hold a solemn[2] supper, sir,
And I'll request your presence.
BAN. Let your highness
Command upon me, to the which my duties
Are with a most indissoluble tie
For ever knit.
MACB. Ride you this afternoon?
BAN. Ay, my good lord.

[1] *all-thing*] altogether.
[2] *solemn*] formal.

MACB. We should have else desired your good advice,
Which still[3] hath been both grave and prosperous,
In this day's council; but we'll take to-morrow.
Is't far you ride?

BAN. As far, my lord, as will fill up the time
'Twixt this and supper: go not my horse the better,
I must become a borrower of the night
For a dark hour or twain.

MACB. Fail not our feast.

BAN. My lord, I will not.

MACB. We hear our bloody cousins are bestow'd
In England and in Ireland, not confessing
Their cruel parricide, filling their hearers
With strange invention: but of that to-morrow,
When therewithal we shall have cause[4] of state
Craving us jointly. Hie you to horse: adieu,
Till you return at night. Goes Fleance with you?

BAN. Ay, my good lord: our time does call upon's.

MACB. I wish your horses swift and sure of foot,
And so I do commend you to their backs.
Farewell. [*Exit Banquo.*
Let every man be master of his time
Till seven at night; to make society
The sweeter welcome, we will keep ourself
Till supper-time alone: while[5] then, God be with you!

[*Exeunt all but Macbeth and an* Attendant.

Sirrah, a word with you: attend those men
Our pleasure?

ATTEND. They are, my lord, without the palace-gate.

MACB. Bring them before us. [*Exit Attendant.*
To be thus is nothing;
But to be safely thus: our fears in Banquo
Stick deep; and in his royalty of nature

[3] *still*] always.
[4] *cause*] affairs.
[5] *while*] until.

Reigns that which would be fear'd: 'tis much he dares,
And, to that dauntless temper of his mind,
He hath a wisdom that doth guide his valour
To act in safety. There is none but he
Whose being I do fear: and under him
My Genius is rebuked, as it is said
Mark Antony's was by Cæsar. He chid the sisters,
When first they put the name of king upon me,
And bade them speak to him; then prophet-like
They hail'd him father to a line of kings:
Upon my head they placed a fruitless crown
And put a barren sceptre in my gripe,
Thence to be wrench'd with an unlineal hand,
No son of mine succeeding. If't be so,
For Banquo's issue have I filed[6] my mind;
For them the gracious Duncan have I murder'd;
Put rancours in the vessel of my peace
Only for them, and mine eternal jewel
Given to the common enemy of man,
To make them kings, the seed of Banquo kings!
Rather than so, come, fate, into the list,
And champion me to the utterance![7] Who's there?

Re-enter Attendant, *with two* Murderers.

Now go to the door, and stay there till we call. [*Exit Attendant.*
Was it not yesterday we spoke together?

FIRST MUR. It was, so please your highness.

MACB. Well then, now
Have you consider'd of my speeches? Know
That it was he in the times past which held you
So under fortune, which you thought had been
Our innocent self: this I made good to you
In our last conference; pass'd in probation with you,
How you were borne in hand,[8] how cross'd, the instruments,
Who wrought with them, and all things else that might

[6] *filed*] defiled.
[7] *utterance*] uttermost.
[8] *borne in hand*] tricked.

To half a soul and to a notion[9] crazed
Say 'Thus did Banquo.'

FIRST MUR. You made it known to us.

MACB. I did so; and went further, which is now
Our point of second meeting. Do you find
Your patience so predominant in your nature,
That you can let this go? Are you so gospell'd,[10]
To pray for this good man and for his issue,
Whose heavy hand hath bow'd you to the grave
And beggar'd yours for ever?

FIRST MUR. We are men, my liege.

MACB. Ay, in the catalogue ye go for men;
As hounds and greyhounds, mongrels, spaniels, curs,
Shoughs, water-rugs[11] and demi-wolves, are clept[12]
All by the name of dogs: the valued file
Distinguishes the swift, the slow, the subtle,
The housekeeper, the hunter, every one
According to the gift which bounteous nature
Hath in him closed, whereby he does receive
Particular addition, from the bill
That writes them all alike: and so of men.
Now if you have a station in the file,
Not i' the worst rank of manhood, say it,
And I will put that business in your bosoms
Whose execution takes your enemy off,
Grapples you to the heart and love of us,
Who wear our health but sickly in his life,
Which in his death were perfect.

SEC. MUR. I am one, my liege,
Whom the vile blows and buffets of the world
Have so incensed that I am reckless what
I do to spite the world.

FIRST MUR. And I another
So weary with disasters, tugg'd with fortune,
That I would set my life on any chance,

[9] *notion*] mind.
[10] *gospell'd*] inclined to act according to the precepts of the Gospels.
[11] *Shoughs, water-rugs*] shaggy dogs, poodles.
[12] *clept*] called.

To mend it or be rid on 't.
MACB. Both of you
Know Banquo was your enemy.
BOTH MUR. True, my lord.
MACB. So is he mine, and in such bloody distance
That every minute of his being thrusts
Against my near'st of life: and though I could
With barefaced power sweep him from my sight
And bid my will avouch it, yet I must not,
For certain friends that are both his and mine,
Whose loves I may not drop, but wail his fall
Who I myself struck down: and thence it is
That I to your assistance do make love,
Masking the business from the common eye
For sundry weighty reasons.
SEC. MUR. We shall, my lord,
Perform what you command us.
FIRST MUR. Though our lives—
MACB. Your spirits shine through you. Within this hour at most
I will advise you where to plant yourselves,
Acquaint you with the perfect spy o' the time,
The moment on 't; for 't must be done to-night,
And something[13] from the palace; always thought
That I require a clearness:[14] and with him—
To leave no rubs nor botches in the work—
Fleance his son, that keeps him company,
Whose absence is no less material to me
Than is his father's, must embrace the fate
Of that dark hour. Resolve yourselves apart:
I'll come to you anon.
BOTH MUR. We are resolved, my lord.
MACB. I'll call upon you straight: abide within. [*Exeunt Murderers.*
It is concluded: Banquo, thy soul's flight,
If it find heaven, must find it out to-night. [*Exit.*

[13] *something*] somewhat.
[14] *clearness*] i.e., alibi.

SCENE II. *The palace.*

Enter LADY MACBETH *and a* Servant.

LADY M. Is Banquo gone from court?
SERV. Ay, madam, but returns again to-night.
LADY M. Say to the king, I would attend his leisure
For a few words.
SERV. Madam, I will. [*Exit.*
LADY M. Nought's had, all's spent,
Where our desire is got without content:
'Tis safer to be that which we destroy
Than by destruction dwell in doubtful joy.

Enter MACBETH.

How now, my lord! why do you keep alone,
Of sorriest fancies your companions making;
Using those thoughts which should indeed have died
With them they think on? Things without all remedy
Should be without regard: what's done is done.
MACB. We have scotch'd[1] the snake, not kill'd it:
She'll close and be herself, whilst our poor malice
Remains in danger of her former tooth.
But let the frame of things disjoint, both the worlds suffer,
Ere we will eat our meal in fear, and sleep
In the affliction of these terrible dreams
That shake us nightly: better be with the dead,
Whom we, to gain our peace, have sent to peace,
Than on the torture of the mind to lie
In restless ecstasy.[2] Duncan is in his grave;
After life's fitful fever he sleeps well;
Treason has done his worst: nor steel, nor poison,
Malice domestic, foreign levy, nothing,
Can touch him further.

[1] *scotch'd*] slashed.
[2] *ecstasy*] mental alienation.

LADY M. Come on;
Gentle my lord, sleek o'er your rugged looks;
Be bright and jovial among your guests to-night.
MACB. So shall I, love; and so, I pray, be you:
Let your remembrance apply to Banquo;
Present him eminence, both with eye and tongue:
Unsafe the while, that we
Must lave our honours in these flattering streams,
And make our faces visards to our hearts,
Disguising what they are.
LADY M. You must leave this.
MACB. O, full of scorpions is my mind, dear wife!
Thou know'st that Banquo, and his Fleance, lives.
LADY M. But in them nature's copy's not eterne.
MACB. There's comfort yet; they are assailable;
Then be thou jocund: ere the bat hath flown
His cloister'd flight; ere to black Hecate's summons
The shard-borne[3] beetle with his drowsy hums
Hath rung night's yawning peal, there shall be done
A deed of dreadful note.
LADY M. What's to be done?
MACB. Be innocent of the knowledge, dearest chuck,
Till thou applaud the deed. Come, seeling[4] night,
Scarf up the tender eye of pitiful day,
And with thy bloody and invisible hand
Cancel and tear to pieces that great bond
Which keeps me pale! Light thickens, and the crow
Makes wing to the rooky wood:
Good things of day begin to droop and drowse,
Whiles night's black agents to their preys do rouse.
Thou marvell'st at my words: but hold thee still;
Things bad begun make strong themselves by ill:
So, prithee, go with me. [*Exeunt.*

[3] *shard-borne*] borne on scaly wings.
[4] *seeling*] blinding. The term, from falconry, refers to the sewing together of the bird's eyelids.

SCENE III. *A park near the palace.*

Enter three Murderers.

FIRST MUR. But who did bid thee join with us?
THIRD MUR. Macbeth.
SEC. MUR. He needs not our mistrust; since he delivers
Our offices, and what we have to do,
To the direction just.[1]
FIRST MUR. Then stand with us.
The west yet glimmers with some streaks of day:
Now spurs the lated[2] traveller apace
To gain the timely inn, and near approaches
The subject of our watch.
THIRD MUR. Hark! I hear horses.
BAN. [*Within*] Give us a light there, ho!
SEC. MUR. Then 'tis he: the rest
That are within the note of expectation[3]
Already are i' the court.
FIRST MUR. His horses go about.
THIRD MUR. Almost a mile: but he does usually—
So all men do—from hence to the palace gate
Make it their walk.
SEC. MUR. A light, a light!

Enter BANQUO, *and* FLEANCE *with a torch*.

THIRD MUR. 'Tis he.
FIRST MUR. Stand to 't.
BAN. It will be rain to-night.
FIRST MUR. Let it come down.
[*They set upon Banquo.*
BAN. O, treachery! Fly, good Fleance, fly, fly, fly!
Thou mayst revenge. O slave! [*Dies. Fleance escapes.*
THIRD MUR. Who did strike out the light?
FIRST MUR. Was't not the way?

[1] *To the direction just*] according to Macbeth's instructions.
[2] *lated*] belated.
[3] *note of expectation*] list of those expected.

THIRD MUR. There's but one down; the son is fled.
SEC. MUR. We have lost
Best half of our affair.
FIRST MUR. Well, let's away and say how much is done. [*Exeunt.*

SCENE IV. *Hall in the palace.*

A banquet prepared. Enter MACBETH, LADY MACBETH, ROSS, LENNOX, Lords, *and* Attendants.

MACB. You know your own degrees; sit down: at first
And last the hearty welcome.
LORDS. Thanks to your majesty.
MACB. Ourself will mingle with society
And play the humble host.
Our hostess keeps her state,[1] but in best time
We will require[2] her welcome.
LADY M. Pronounce it for me, sir, to all our friends,
For my heart speaks they are welcome.

Enter first Murderer *to the door.*

MACB. See, they encounter thee with their hearts' thanks.
Both sides are even: here I'll sit i' the midst:
Be large[3] in mirth; anon we'll drink a measure
The table round. [*Approaching the door*] There's blood upon thy face.
MUR. 'Tis Banquo's then.
MACB. 'Tis better thee without than he within.
Is he dispatch'd?
MUR. My lord, his throat is cut; that I did for him.
MACB. Thou art the best o' the cut-throats: yet he's good
That did the like for Fleance: if thou didst it,

[1] *state*] canopied chair of state.
[2] *require*] request.
[3] *large*] liberal.

Thou art the nonpareil.[4]

MUR. Most royal sir,
Fleance is 'scaped.

MACB. [*Aside*] Then comes my fit again: I had else been perfect,
Whole as the marble, founded as the rock,
As broad and general as the casing air:[5]
But now I am cabin'd, cribb'd,[6] confined, bound in
To saucy[7] doubts and fears.—But Banquo's safe?

MUR. Ay, my good lord: safe in a ditch he bides,
With twenty trenched[8] gashes on his head;
The least a death to nature.

MACB. Thanks for that.
[*Aside*] There the grown serpent lies; the worm[9] that's fled
Hath nature that in time will venom breed,
No teeth for the present. Get thee gone: to-morrow
We'll hear ourselves again.[10] [*Exit Murderer.*

LADY M. My royal lord,
You do not give the cheer: the feast is sold
That is not often vouch'd,[11] while 'tis a-making,
'Tis given with welcome: to feed were best at home;
From thence[12] the sauce to meat is ceremony;
Meeting were bare without it.

MACB. Sweet remembrancer!
Now good digestion wait on appetite,
And health on both!

LEN. May't please your highness sit.

[*The Ghost of Banquo enters, and sits in Macbeth's place.*

MACB. Here had we now our country's honour roof'd,
Were the graced[13] person of our Banquo present;

[4] *nonpareil*] paragon.
[5] *broad . . . air*] free and unrestrained as the surrounding air.
[6] *cribb'd*] caged.
[7] *saucy*] unbounded.
[8] *trenched*] cut.
[9] *worm*] serpent.
[10] *hear ourselves again*] discuss things further.
[11] *vouch'd*] asserted.
[12] *From thence*] away from home.
[13] *graced*] dignified.

Who may I rather challenge for unkindness
Than pity for mischance!

ROSS. His absence, sir,
Lays blame upon his promise. Please't your highness
To grace us with your royal company.

MACB. The table's full.

LEN. Here is a place reserved, sir.

MACB. Where?

LEN. Here, my good lord. What is't that moves your highness?

MACB. Which of you have done this?

LORDS. What, my good lord?

MACB. Thou canst not say I did it: never shake
Thy gory locks at me.

ROSS. Gentlemen, rise; his highness is not well.

LADY M. Sit, worthy friends: my lord is often thus,
And hath been from his youth: pray you, keep seat;
The fit is momentary; upon a thought[14]
He will again be well: if much you note him,
You shall offend him and extend his passion:
Feed, and regard him not. Are you a man?

MACB. Ay, and a bold one, that dare look on that
Which might appal the devil.

LADY M. O proper stuff!
This is the very painting of your fear:
This is the air-drawn dagger which, you said,
Led you to Duncan. O, these flaws[15] and starts,
Impostors to true fear, would well become
A woman's story at a winter's fire,
Authorized by her grandam. Shame itself!
Why do you make such faces? When all's done,
You look but on a stool.

MACB. Prithee, see there! behold! look! lo! how say you?
Why, what care I? If thou canst nod, speak too.
If charnel-houses and our graves must send
Those that we bury back, our monuments
Shall be the maws of kites. [*Exit Ghost.*

[14] *upon a thought*] in no time.
[15] *flaws*] storms of passion.

LADY M. What, quite unmann'd in folly?
MACB. If I stand here, I saw him.
LADY M. Fie, for shame!
MACB. Blood hath been shed ere now, i' the olden time,
Ere humane statute purged the gentle weal;
Ay, and since too, murders have been perform'd
Too terrible for the ear: the time has been,
That, when the brains were out, the man would die,
And there an end; but now they rise again,
With twenty mortal murders[16] on their crowns,
And push us from our stools: this is more strange
Than such a murder is.
LADY M. My worthy lord,
Your noble friends do lack you.
MACB. I do forget.
Do not muse at me, my most worthy friends;
I have a strange infirmity, which is nothing
To those that know me. Come, love and health to all;
Then I'll sit down. Give me some wine, fill full.
I drink to the general joy o' the whole table,
And to our dear friend Banquo, whom we miss;
Would he were here! to all and him we thirst,
And all to all.
LORDS. Our duties, and the pledge.

Re-enter Ghost.

MACB. Avaunt! and quit my sight! let the earth hide thee!
Thy bones are marrowless, thy blood is cold;
Thou hast no speculation[17] in those eyes
Which thou dost glare with.
LADY M. Think of this, good peers,
But as a thing of custom: 'tis no other;
Only it spoils the pleasure of the time.
MACB. What man dare, I dare:
Approach thou like the rugged Russian bear,
The arm'd rhinoceros, or the Hyrcan tiger;

[16] *mortal murders*] fatal wounds.
[17] *speculation*] power of intelligent vision.

Take any shape but that, and my firm nerves
Shall never tremble: or be alive again,
And dare me to the desert with thy sword;
If trembling I inhabit then, protest me
The baby of a girl. Hence, horrible shadow!
Unreal mockery, hence! [*Exit Ghost.*
Why, so: being gone,
I am a man again. Pray you, sit still.

LADY M. You have displaced the mirth, broke the good meeting,
With most admired disorder.[18]

MACB. Can such things be,
And overcome[19] us like a summer's cloud,
Without our special wonder? You make me strange
Even to the disposition that I owe,[20]
When now I think you can behold such sights,
And keep the natural ruby of your cheeks,
When mine is blanch'd with fear.

ROSS. What sights, my lord?

LADY M. I pray you, speak not; he grows worse and worse;
Question enrages him: at once, good night:
Stand not upon the order of your going,
But go at once.

LEN. Good night; and better health
Attend his majesty!

LADY M. A kind good night to all!

[*Exeunt all but Macbeth and Lady M.*

MACB. It will have blood: they say blood will have blood:
Stones have been known to move and trees to speak;
Augures[21] and understood relations have
By maggot-pies[22] and choughs and rooks brought forth
The secret'st man of blood. What is the night?

LADY M. Almost at odds with morning, which is which.

MACB. How say'st thou, that Macduff denies his person

[18] *admired disorder*] amazing mental derangement.
[19] *overcome*] pass over.
[20] *owe*] possess.
[21] *Augures*] auguries.
[22] *maggot-pies*] magpies.

At our great bidding?
LADY M. Did you send to him, sir?
MACB. I hear it by the way, but I will send:
There's not a one of them but in his house
I keep a servant fee'd. I will to-morrow,
And betimes I will, to the weird sisters:
More shall they speak, for now I am bent to know,
By the worst means, the worst. For mine own good
All causes shall give way: I am in blood
Stepp'd in so far that, should I wade no more,
Returning were as tedious as go o'er:
Strange things I have in head that will to hand,
Which must be acted ere they may be scann'd.
LADY M. You lack the season of all natures, sleep.
MACB. Come, we'll to sleep. My strange and self-abuse[23]
Is the initiate fear[24] that wants hard use:
We are yet but young in deed. [*Exeunt.*

SCENE V. *A heath.*

Thunder. Enter the three Witches, *meeting* HECATE.

FIRST WITCH. Why, how now, Hecate! you look angerly.
HEC. Have I not reason, beldams as you are,
Saucy and over-bold? How did you dare
To trade and traffic with Macbeth
In riddles and affairs of death;
And I, the mistress of your charms,
The close contriver of all harms,
Was never call'd to bear my part,
Or show the glory of our art?
And, which is worse, all you have done
Hath been but for a wayward son,
Spiteful and wrathful; who, as others do,

[23] *self-abuse*] delusion.
[24] *initiate fear*] novice's fear.

Loves for his own ends, not for you.
But make amends now: get you gone,
And at the pit of Acheron
Meet me i' the morning: thither he
Will come to know his destiny:
Your vessels and your spells provide,
Your charms and every thing beside.
I am for the air; this night I'll spend
Unto a dismal[1] and a fatal end:
Great business must be wrought ere noon:
Upon the corner of the moon
There hangs a vaporous drop profound;
I'll catch it ere it come to ground:
And that distill'd by magic sleights
Shall raise such artificial[2] sprites
As by the strength of their illusion
Shall draw him on to his confusion:
He shall spurn fate, scorn death, and bear
His hopes 'bove wisdom, grace and fear:
And you all know security[3]
Is mortals' chiefest enemy.

[*Music and a song within*: 'Come away, come away,' &c.

Hark! I am call'd; my little spirit, see,
Sits in a foggy cloud, and stays for me. [*Exit*.

FIRST WITCH. Come, let's make haste; she'll soon be back again. [*Exeunt*.

SCENE VI. *Forres. The palace.*

Enter LENNOX *and another* Lord.

LEN. My former speeches have but hit your thoughts,
Which can interpret farther: only I say

[1] *dismal*] disastrous.
[2] *artificial*] artful, cunning.
[3] *security*] overconfidence, carelessness.

Things have been strangely borne.[1] The gracious Duncan
Was pitied of Macbeth: marry, he was dead:
And the right-valiant Banquo walk'd too late;
Whom, you may say, if't please you, Fleance kill'd,
For Fleance fled: men must not walk too late.
Who cannot want the thought, how monstrous
It was for Malcolm and for Donalbain
To kill their gracious father? damned fact![2]
How it did grieve Macbeth! did he not straight,
In pious rage, the two delinquents tear,
That were the slaves of drink and thralls of sleep?
Was not that nobly done? Ay, and wisely too;
For 'twould have anger'd any heart alive
To hear the men deny't. So that, I say,
He has borne all things well: and I do think
That, had he Duncan's sons under his key—
As, an't please heaven, he shall not—they should find
What 'twere to kill a father; so should Fleance.
But, peace! for from broad words, and 'cause he fail'd
His presence at the tyrant's feast, I hear,
Macduff lives in disgrace: sir, can you tell
Where he bestows himself?

LORD. The son of Duncan,
From whom this tyrant holds the due of birth,
Lives in the English court, and is received
Of the most pious Edward with such grace
That the malevolence of fortune nothing
Takes from his high respect. Thither Macduff
Is gone to pray the holy king, upon his aid
To wake Northumberland and warlike Siward:
That by the help of these, with Him above
To ratify the work, we may again
Give to our tables meat, sleep to our nights,
Free from our feasts and banquets bloody knives,
Do faithful homage and receive free honours:
All which we pine for now: and this report

[1] *borne*] conducted.
[2] *fact*] deed.

Hath so exasperate the king that he
Prepares for some attempt of war.

LEN. Sent he to Macduff?

LORD. He did: and with an absolute 'Sir, not I,'
The cloudy[3] messenger turns me his back,
And hums, as who should say 'You'll rue the time
That clogs me with this answer.'

LEN. And that well might
Advise him to a caution, to hold what distance
His wisdom can provide. Some holy angel
Fly to the court of England and unfold
His message ere he come, that a swift blessing
May soon return to this our suffering country
Under a hand accursed!

LORD. I'll send my prayers with him.

[*Exeunt.*

[3] *cloudy*] morose.

ACT IV.

SCENE I. *A cavern. In the middle, a boiling cauldron.*

Thunder. Enter the three Witches.

FIRST WITCH. Thrice the brinded[1] cat hath mew'd.
SEC. WITCH. Thrice and once the hedge-pig[2] whined.
THIRD WITCH. Harpier cries ' 'Tis time, 'tis time.'
FIRST WITCH. Round about the cauldron go:
In the poison'd entrails throw.
Toad, that under cold stone
Days and nights has thirty one
Swelter'd[3] venom sleeping got,
Boil thou first i' the charmed pot.
ALL. Double, double toil and trouble;
Fire burn and cauldron bubble.
SEC. WITCH. Fillet of a fenny snake,
In the cauldron boil and bake;
Eye of newt and toe of frog,
Wool of bat and tongue of dog,
Adder's fork[4] and blind-worm's sting,
Lizard's leg and howlet's wing,
For a charm of powerful trouble,
Like a hell-broth boil and bubble.
ALL. Double, double toil and trouble;
Fire burn and cauldron bubble.
THIRD WITCH. Scale of dragon, tooth of wolf,

[1] *brinded*] spotted, brindled.
[2] *hedge-pig*] hedgehog.
[3] *Swelter'd*] exuded.
[4] *fork*] forked tongue.

Witches' mummy, maw and gulf[5]
Of the ravin'd salt-sea shark,
Root of hemlock digg'd i' the dark,
Liver of blaspheming Jew,
Gall of goat and slips of yew
Sliver'd[6] in the moon's eclipse,
Nose of Turk and Tartar's lips,
Finger of birth-strangled babe
Ditch-deliver'd by a drab,
Make the gruel thick and slab:[7]
Add thereto a tiger's chaudron,[8]
For the ingredients of our cauldron.

ALL. Double, double toil and trouble;
Fire burn and cauldron bubble.

SEC. WITCH. Cool it with a baboon's blood,
Then the charm is firm and good.

Enter HECATE *to the other three* Witches.

HEC. O, well done! I commend your pains;
And every one shall share i' the gains:
And now about the cauldron sing,
Like elves and fairies in a ring,
Enchanting all that you put in.
[*Music and a song*: 'Black spirits,' &c.
[*Hecate retires.*

SEC. WITCH. By the pricking of my thumbs,
Something wicked this way comes:
Open, locks,
Whoever knocks!

Enter MACBETH.

MACB. How now, you secret, black, and midnight hags!
What is't you do?

ALL. A deed without a name.

[5] *gulf*] gullet.
[6] *Sliver'd*] broken off.
[7] *slab*] glutinous.
[8] *chaudron*] entrails.

MACB. I conjure you, by that which you profess,
Howe'er you come to know it, answer me:
Though you untie the winds and let them fight
Against the churches; though the yesty[9] waves
Confound and swallow navigation up;
Though bladed corn be lodged[10] and trees blown down;
Though castles topple on their warders' heads;
Though palaces and pyramids do slope
Their heads to their foundations; though the treasure
Of nature's germens[11] tumble all together,
Even till destruction sicken; answer me
To what I ask you.

FIRST WITCH. Speak.

SEC. WITCH. Demand.

THIRD WITCH. We'll answer.

FIRST WITCH. Say, if thou'dst rather hear it from our mouths,
Or from our masters?

MACB. Call 'em, let me see 'em.

FIRST WITCH. Pour in sow's blood, that hath eaten
Her nine farrow;[12] grease that's sweaten
From the murderer's gibbet throw
Into the flame.

ALL. Come, high or low;
Thyself and office deftly show!

Thunder. First Apparition: *an armed Head.*

MACB. Tell me, thou unknown power,—

FIRST WITCH. He knows thy thought:
Hear his speech, but say thou nought.

FIRST APP. Macbeth! Macbeth! Macbeth! beware Macduff;
Beware the thane of Fife. Dismiss me: enough. [*Descends.*

MACB. Whate'er thou art, for thy good caution thanks;
Thou hast harp'd[13] my fear aright: but one word more,—

FIRST WITCH. He will not be commanded: here's another,

[9] *yesty*] foamy.
[10] *lodged*] beaten flat.
[11] *germens*] seeds.
[12] *farrow*] litter.
[13] *harp'd*] hit upon.

More potent than the first.

Thunder. Second Apparition: *a bloody Child.*

SEC. APP. Macbeth! Macbeth! Macbeth!
MACB. Had I three ears, I'ld hear thee.
SEC. APP. Be bloody, bold and resolute; laugh to scorn
The power of man, for none of woman born
Shall harm Macbeth. [*Descends.*
MACB. Then live, Macduff: what need I fear of thee?
But yet I'll make assurance double sure,
And take a bond of fate: thou shalt not live;
That I may tell pale-hearted fear it lies,
And sleep in spite of thunder.

Thunder. Third Apparition: *a Child crowned, with a tree in his hand.*

What is this,
That rises like the issue of a king,
And wears upon his baby-brow the round
And top of sovereignty?
ALL. Listen, but speak not to't.
THIRD APP. Be lion-mettled, proud, and take no care
Who chafes, who frets, or where conspirers are:
Macbeth shall never vanquish'd be until
Great Birnam wood to high Dunsinane hill
Shall come against him. [*Descends.*
MACB. That will never be:
Who can impress the forest, bid the tree
Unfix his earth-bound root? Sweet bodements! good!
Rebellion's head, rise never, till the wood
Of Birnam rise, and our high-placed Macbeth
Shall live the lease of nature, pay his breath
To time and mortal custom. Yet my heart
Throbs to know one thing: tell me, if your art
Can tell so much: shall Banquo's issue ever
Reign in this kingdom?
ALL. Seek to know no more.
MACB. I will be satisfied: deny me this,
And an eternal curse fall on you! Let me know:

Why sinks that cauldron? and what noise[14] is this? [*Hautboys.*
FIRST WITCH. Show!
SEC. WITCH. Show!
THIRD WITCH. Show!
ALL. Show his eyes, and grieve his heart;
Come like shadows, so depart!

A show of eight Kings, *the last with a glass in his hand; Banquo's Ghost following.*

MACB. Thou art too like the spirit of Banquo: down!
Thy crown does sear mine eye-balls. And thy hair,
Thou other gold-bound brow, is like the first.
A third is like the former. Filthy hags!
Why do you show me this? A fourth! Start, eyes!
What, will the line stretch out to the crack of doom?
Another yet! A seventh! I'll see no more:
And yet the eighth appears, who bears a glass
Which shows me many more; and some I see
That two-fold balls and treble sceptres carry:
Horrible sight! Now I see 'tis true;
For the blood-bolter'd[15] Banquo smiles upon me,
And points at them for his. What, is this so?
FIRST WITCH. Ay, sir, all this is so: but why
Stands Macbeth thus amazedly?
Come, sisters, cheer we up his sprites,
And show the best of our delights:
I'll charm the air to give a sound,
While you perform your antic round,[16]
That this great king may kindly say
Our duties did his welcome pay.

[*Music. The Witches dance, and then vanish, with Hecate.*

MACB. Where are they? Gone? Let this pernicious hour
Stand aye accursed in the calendar!
Come in, without there!

[14] *noise*] music.
[15] *blood-bolter'd*] with blood-clotted hair.
[16] *antic round*] old and fantastic dance.

Enter LENNOX.

LEN. What's your grace's will?
MACB. Saw you the weird sisters?
LEN. No, my lord.
MACB. Came they not by you?
LEN. No indeed, my lord.
MACB. Infected be the air whereon they ride,
And damn'd all those that trust them! I did hear
The galloping of horse: who was't came by?
LEN. 'Tis two or three, my lord, that bring you word
Macduff is fled to England.
MACB. Fled to England!
LEN. Ay, my good lord.
MACB. [*Aside*] Time, thou anticipatest my dread exploits:
The flighty purpose never is o'ertook
Unless the deed go with it: from this moment
The very firstlings of my heart shall be
The firstlings of my hand. And even now,
To crown my thoughts with acts, be it thought and done:
The castle of Macduff I will surprise;
Seize upon Fife; give to the edge o' the sword
His wife, his babes, and all unfortunate souls
That trace him in his line. No boasting like a fool;
This deed I'll do before this purpose cool:
But no more sights!—Where are these gentlemen?
Come, bring me where they are. [*Exeunt.*

SCENE II. *Fife. Macduff's castle.*

Enter LADY MACDUFF, *her* SON, *and* ROSS.

L. MACD. What had he done, to make him fly the land?
ROSS. You must have patience, madam.
L. MACD. He had none:
His flight was madness: when our actions do not,
Our fears do make us traitors.

ROSS. You know not
Whether it was his wisdom or his fear.
L. MACD. Wisdom! to leave his wife, to leave his babes,
His mansion and his titles,[1] in a place
From whence himself does fly? He loves us not;
He wants the natural touch:[2] for the poor wren,
The most diminutive of birds, will fight,
Her young ones in her nest, against the owl.
All is the fear and nothing is the love;
As little is the wisdom, where the flight
So runs against all reason.
ROSS. My dearest coz,
I pray you, school[3] yourself: but, for your husband,
He is noble, wise, judicious, and best knows
The fits o' the season. I dare not speak much further:
But cruel are the times, when we are traitors
And do not know ourselves; when we hold rumour
From what we fear, yet know not what we fear,
But float upon a wild and violent sea
Each way and move. I take my leave of you:
Shall not be long but I'll be here again:
Things at the worst will cease, or else climb upward
To what they were before. My pretty cousin,
Blessing upon you!
L. MACD. Father'd he is, and yet he's fatherless.
ROSS. I am so much a fool, should I stay longer,
It would be my disgrace and your discomfort:
I take my leave at once. [*Exit.*

L. MACD. Sirrah, your father's dead:
And what will you do now? How will you live?
SON. As birds do, mother.
L. MACD. What, with worms and flies?
SON. With what I get, I mean; and so do they.
L. MACD. Poor bird! thou'ldst never fear the net nor lime,
The pitfall nor the gin.
SON. Why should I, mother? Poor birds they are not set for.

[1] *titles*] possessions.
[2] *touch*] feeling, affection.
[3] *school*] control.

My father is not dead, for all your saying.
L. MACD. Yes, he is dead: how wilt thou do for a father?
SON. Nay, how will you do for a husband?
L. MACD. Why, I can buy me twenty at any market.
SON. Then you'll buy 'em to sell again.
L. MACD. Thou speak'st with all thy wit, and yet, i' faith,
With wit enough for thee.
SON. Was my father a traitor, mother?
L. MACD. Ay, that he was.
SON. What is a traitor?
L. MACD. Why, one that swears and lies.
SON. And be all traitors that do so?
L. MACD. Every one that does so is a traitor, and must be hanged.
SON. And must they all be hanged that swear and lie?
L. MACD. Every one.
SON. Who must hang them?
L. MACD. Why, the honest men.
SON. Then the liars and swearers are fools; for there are liars and swearers enow to beat the honest men and hang up them.
L. MACD. Now, God help thee, poor monkey! But how wilt thou do for a father?
SON. If he were dead, you'ld weep for him: if you would not, it were a good sign that I should quickly have a new father.
L. MACD. Poor prattler, how thou talk'st!

Enter a Messenger.

MESS. Bless you, fair dame! I am not to you known,
Though, in your state of honour I am perfect.[4]
I doubt[5] some danger does approach you nearly:
If you will take a homely man's advice,
Be not found here; hence, with your little ones.
To fright you thus, methinks I am too savage;
To do worse to you were fell cruelty,
Which is too nigh your person. Heaven preserve you!
I dare abide no longer. *Exit.*
L. MACD. Whither should I fly?

[4] *perfect*] fully aware.
[5] *doubt*] fear.

I have done no harm. But I remember now
I am in this earthly world, where to do harm
Is often laudable, to do good sometime
Accounted dangerous folly: why then, alas,
Do I put up that womanly defence,
To say I have done no harm?—What are these faces?

Enter Murderers.

FIRST MUR. Where is your husband?
L. MACD. I hope, in no place so unsanctified
Where such as thou mayst find him.
FIRST MUR. He's a traitor.
SON. Thou liest, thou shag-ear'd villain!
FIRST MUR. What, you egg!
[*Stabbing him.*
Young fry of treachery!
SON. He has kill'd me, mother:
Run away, I pray you! [*Dies.*
[*Exit Lady Macduff, crying* 'Murder!'
[*Exeunt murderers, following her.*

SCENE III. *England. Before the King's palace.*

Enter MALCOLM *and* MACDUFF.

MAL. Let us seek out some desolate shade, and there
Weep our sad bosoms empty.
MACD. Let us rather
Hold fast the mortal sword, and like good men
Bestride our down-fall'n birthdom:[1] each new morn
New widows howl, new orphans cry, new sorrows
Strike heaven on the face, that it resounds
As if it felt with Scotland and yell'd out
Like syllable of dolour.

[1] *birthdom*] motherland.

MAL. What I believe, I'll wail;
What know, believe; and what I can redress,
As I shall find the time to friend, I will.
What you have spoke, it may be so perchance.
This tyrant, whose sole name blisters our tongues,
Was once thought honest: you have loved him well;
He hath not touch'd you yet. I am young; but something
You may deserve of him through me; and wisdom
To offer up a weak, poor, innocent lamb
To appease an angry god.
MACD. I am not treacherous.
MAL. But Macbeth is.
A good and virtuous nature may recoil
In an imperial charge.[2] But I shall crave your pardon;
That which you are, my thoughts cannot transpose:[3]
Angels are bright still, though the brightest fell:
Though all things foul would wear the brows of grace,
Yet grace must still look so.
MACD. I have lost my hopes.
MAL. Perchance even there where I did find my doubts.
Why in that rawness[4] left you wife and child,
Those precious motives, those strong knots of love,
Without leave-taking? I pray you,
Let not my jealousies[5] be your dishonours,
But mine own safeties. You may be rightly just,
Whatever I shall think.
MACD. Bleed, bleed, poor country:
Great tyranny, lay thou thy basis sure,
For goodness dare not check thee: wear thou thy wrongs;
The title is affeer'd.[6] Fare thee well, lord:
I would not be the villain that thou think'st
For the whole space that's in the tyrant's grasp
And the rich East to boot.
MAL. Be not offended:

[2] *charge*] command.
[3] *transpose*] alter.
[4] *rawness*] exposed condition.
[5] *jealousies*] suspicions.
[6] *affeer'd*] confirmed.

I speak not as in absolute fear of you.
I think our country sinks beneath the yoke;
It weeps, it bleeds, and each new day a gash
Is added to her wounds: I think withal
There would be hands uplifted in my right;
And here from gracious England[7] have I offer
Of goodly thousands: but for all this,
When I shall tread upon the tyrant's head,
Or wear it on my sword, yet my poor country
Shall have more vices than it had before,
More suffer and more sundry ways than ever,
By him that shall succeed.

MACD. What should he be?

MAL. It is myself I mean: in whom I know
All the particulars of vice so grafted
That, when they shall be open'd, black Macbeth
Will seem as pure as snow, and the poor state
Esteem him as a lamb, being compared
With my confineless[8] harms.

MACD. Not in the legions
Of horrid hell can come a devil more damn'd
In evils to top Macbeth.

MAL. I grant him bloody,
Luxurious,[9] avaricious, false, deceitful,
Sudden,[10] malicious, smacking of every sin
That has a name: but there's no bottom, none,
In my voluptuousness: your wives, your daughters,
Your matrons and your maids, could not fill up
The cistern of my lust, and my desire
All continent[11] impediments would o'erbear,
That did oppose my will: better Macbeth
Than such an one to reign.

MACD. Boundless intemperance

[7] *England*] the King of England.
[8] *confineless*] boundless.
[9] *Luxurious*] lascivious.
[10] *Sudden*] violent, impetuous.
[11] *continent*] restraining, chaste.

In nature[12] is a tyranny; it hath been
The untimely emptying of the happy throne,
And fall of many kings. But fear not yet
To take upon you what is yours: you may
Convey[13] your pleasures in a spacious plenty,
And yet seem cold, the time you may so hoodwink:
We have willing dames enough; there cannot be
That vulture in you, to devour so many
As will to greatness dedicate themselves,
Finding it so inclined.

MAL. With this there grows
In my most ill-composed affection[14] such
A stanchless[15] avarice that, were I king,
I should cut off the nobles for their lands,
Desire his[16] jewels and this other's house:
And my more-having would be as a sauce
To make me hunger more, that I should forge
Quarrels unjust against the good and loyal,
Destroying them for wealth.

MACD. This avarice
Sticks deeper, grows with more pernicious root
Than summer-seeming[17] lust, and it hath been
The sword of our slain kings: yet do not fear;
Scotland hath foisons[18] to fill up your will
Of your mere own: all these are portable,
With other graces weigh'd.[19]

MAL. But I have none: the king-becoming graces,
As justice, verity, temperance, stableness,
Bounty, perseverance, mercy, lowliness,
Devotion, patience, courage, fortitude,
I have no relish[20] of them, but abound

[12] *nature*] natural appetites.
[13] *Convey*] carry out secretly.
[14] *affection*] disposition.
[15] *stanchless*] insatiable.
[16] *his*] one person's.
[17] *summer-seeming*] summer-like, transitory.
[18] *foisons*] rich harvests, plenty.
[19] *weigh'd*] counterbalanced.
[20] *relish*] trace.

In the division[21] of each several crime,
Acting it many ways. Nay, had I power, I should
Pour the sweet milk of concord into hell,
Uproar[22] the universal peace, confound
All unity on earth.

MACD. O Scotland, Scotland!

MAL. If such a one be fit to govern, speak:
I am as I have spoken.

MACD. Fit to govern!
No, not to live. O nation miserable!
With an untitled tyrant bloody-scepter'd,
When shalt thou see thy wholesome days again,
Since that the truest issue of thy throne
By his own interdiction stands accursed,
And does blaspheme[23] his breed? Thy royal father
Was a most sainted king: the queen that bore thee,
Oftener upon her knees than on her feet,
Died every day she lived. Fare thee well!
These evils thou repeat'st upon thyself
Have banish'd me from Scotland. O my breast,
Thy hope ends here!

MAL. Macduff, this noble passion,
Child of integrity, hath from my soul
Wiped the black scruples, reconciled my thoughts
To thy good truth and honour. Devilish Macbeth
By many of these trains[24] hath sought to win me
Into his power; and modest wisdom plucks me
From over-credulous haste: but God above
Deal between thee and me! for even now
I put myself to thy direction, and
Unspeak mine own detraction; here abjure
The taints and blames I laid upon myself,
For strangers to my nature. I am yet
Unknown to woman, never was forsworn,
Scarcely have coveted what was mine own,

[21] *division*] variation.
[22] *Uproar*] disturb.
[23] *blaspheme*] slander.
[24] *trains*] stratagems, lures.

At no time broke my faith, would not betray
The devil to his fellow, and delight
No less in truth than life: my first false speaking
Was this upon myself: what I am truly,
Is thine and my poor country's to command:
Whither indeed, before thy here-approach,
Old Siward, with ten thousand warlike men,
Already at a point,[25] was setting forth.
Now we'll together, and the chance of goodness[26]
Be like our warranted quarrel! Why are you silent?

MACD. Such welcome and unwelcome things at once
'Tis hard to reconcile.

Enter a Doctor.

MAL. Well, more anon. Comes the king forth, I pray you?

DOCT. Ay, sir; there are a crew of wretched souls
That stay his cure: their malady convinces[27]
The great assay of art; but at his touch,
Such sanctity hath heaven given his hand,
They presently amend.

MAL. I thank you, doctor. [*Exit Doctor.*

MACD. What's the disease he means?

MAL. 'Tis call'd the evil:[28]
A most miraculous work in this good king;
Which often, since my here-remain in England,
I have seen him do. How he solicits heaven,
Himself best knows: but strangely-visited people,
All swoln and ulcerous, pitiful to the eye,
The mere[29] despair of surgery, he cures,
Hanging a golden stamp[30] about their necks,
Put on with holy prayers: and 'tis spoken,
To the succeeding royalty he leaves
The healing benediction. With this strange virtue
He hath a heavenly gift of prophecy,

[25] *at a point*] prepared.
[26] *goodness*] good fortune.
[27] *convinces*] conquers.
[28] *the evil*] i.e., the king's evil (scrofula).
[29] *mere*] absolute.
[30] *stamp*] coin.

And sundry blessings hang about his throne
That speak him full of grace.

Enter ROSS.

MACD. See, who comes here?
MAL. My countryman; but yet I know him not.
MACD. My ever gentle cousin, welcome hither.
MAL. I know him now: good God, betimes remove
The means that makes us strangers!
ROSS. Sir, amen.
MACD. Stands Scotland where it did?
ROSS. Alas, poor country!
Almost afraid to know itself! It cannot
Be call'd our mother, but our grave: where nothing,
But who knows nothing, is once[31] seen to smile;
Where sighs and groans and shrieks that rend the air,
Are made, not mark'd; where violent sorrow seems
A modern ecstasy:[32] the dead man's knell
Is there scarce ask'd for who; and good men's lives
Expire before the flowers in their caps,
Dying or ere they sicken.
MACD. O, relation
Too nice,[33] and yet too true!
MAL. What's the newest grief?
ROSS. That of an hour's age doth hiss the speaker;
Each minute teems a new one.
MACD. How does my wife?
ROSS. Why, well.
MACD. And all my children?
ROSS. Well too.
MACD. The tyrant has not batter'd at their peace?
ROSS. No; they were well at peace when I did leave 'em.
MACD. Be not a niggard of your speech: how goes't?
ROSS. When I came hither to transport the tidings,
Which I have heavily borne, there ran a rumour
Of many worthy fellows that were out;[34]

[31] *once*] ever.
[32] *modern ecstasy*] common emotion.
[33] *nice*] precise.
[34] *out*] in rebellion.

Which was to my belief witness'd the rather,
For that I saw the tyrant's power a-foot:
Now is the time of help; your eye in Scotland
Would create soldiers, make our women fight,
To doff their dire distresses.

MAL. Be't their comfort
We are coming thither: gracious England hath
Lent us good Siward and ten thousand men;
An older and a better soldier none
That Christendom gives out.[35]

ROSS. Would I could answer
This comfort with the like! But I have words
That would be howl'd out in the desert air,
Where hearing should not latch[36] them.

MACD. What concern they?
The general cause? or is it a fee-grief[37]
Due to some single breast?

ROSS. No mind that's honest
But in it shares some woe, though the main part
Pertains to you alone.

MACD. If it be mine,
Keep it not from me, quickly let me have it.

ROSS. Let not your ears despise my tongue for ever,
Which shall possess[38] them with the heaviest sound
That ever yet they heard.

MACD. Hum! I guess at it.

ROSS. Your castle is surprised; your wife and babes
Savagely slaughter'd: to relate the manner,
Were, on the quarry of these murder'd deer,
To add the death of you.

MAL. Merciful heaven!
What, man! ne'er pull your hat upon your brows;
Give sorrow words: the grief that does not speak
Whispers the o'er-fraught heart, and bids it break.

MACD. My children too?

[35] *gives out*] proclaims.
[36] *latch*] catch.
[37] *fee-grief*] grief pertaining to an individual.
[38] *possess*] fill.

ROSS. Wife, children, servants, all
That could be found.
MACD. And I must be from thence!
My wife kill'd too?
ROSS. I have said.
MAL. Be comforted:
Let's make us medicines of our great revenge,
To cure this deadly grief.
MACD. He has no children. All my pretty ones?
Did you say all? O hell-kite! All?
What, all my pretty chickens and their dam
At one fell swoop?
MAL. Dispute it like a man.
MACD. I shall do so;
But I must also feel it as a man:
I cannot but remember such things were,
That were most precious to me. Did heaven look on,
And would not take their part? Sinful Macduff,
They were all struck for thee! naught[39] that I am,
Not for their own demerits, but for mine,
Fell slaughter on their souls: heaven rest them now!
MAL. Be this the whetstone of your sword: let grief
Convert to anger; blunt not the heart, enrage it.
MACD. O, I could play the woman with mine eyes,
And braggart with my tongue! But, gentle heavens,
Cut short all intermission; front to front
Bring thou this fiend of Scotland and myself;
Within my sword's length set him; if he 'scape,
Heaven forgive him too!
MAL. This tune goes manly.
Come, go we to the king; our power[40] is ready;
Our lack is nothing but our leave.[41] Macbeth
Is ripe for shaking, and the powers above
Put on their instruments. Receive what cheer you may;
The night is long that never finds the day. [*Exeunt*.

[39] *naught*] wicked.
[40] *power*] army.
[41] *leave*] leave-taking.

ACT V.

SCENE I. *Dunsinane. Ante-room in the castle.*

Enter a Doctor of Physic *and a* Waiting-Gentlewoman.

DOCT. I have two nights watched with you, but can perceive no truth in your report. When was it she last walked?

GENT. Since his majesty went into the field, I have seen her rise from her bed, throw her nightgown upon her, unlock her closet, take forth paper, fold it, write upon 't, read it, afterwards seal it, and again return to bed; yet all this while in a most fast sleep.

DOCT. A great perturbation in nature, to receive at once the benefit of sleep and do the effects of watching! In this slumbery agitation, besides her walking and other actual performances, what, at any time, have you heard her say?

GENT. That, sir, which I will not report after her.

DOCT. You may to me, and 'tis most meet you should.

GENT. Neither to you nor any one, having no witness to confirm my speech.

Enter LADY MACBETH, *with a taper.*

Lo you, here she comes! This is her very guise, and, upon my life, fast asleep. Observe her; stand close.[1]

DOCT. How came she by that light?

GENT. Why, it stood by her: she has light by her continually; 'tis her command.

DOCT. You see, her eyes are open.

GENT. Ay, but their sense is shut.

DOCT. What is it she does now? Look, how she rubs her hands.

[1] *close*] hidden.

GENT. It is an accustomed action with her, to seem thus washing her hands: I have known her continue in this a quarter of an hour.

LADY M. Yet here's a spot.

DOCT. Hark! she speaks: I will set down what comes from her, to satisfy my remembrance the more strongly.

LADY M. Out, damned spot! out, I say! One: two: why, then 'tis time to do't. Hell is murky. Fie, my lord, fie! a soldier, and afeard? What need we fear who knows it, when none can call our power to account? Yet who would have thought the old man to have had so much blood in him?

DOCT. Do you mark that?

LADY M. The thane of Fife had a wife; where is she now? What, will these hands ne'er be clean? No more o' that, my lord, no more o' that: you mar all with this starting.

DOCT. Go to, go to; you have known what you should not.

GENT. She has spoke what she should not, I am sure of that: heaven knows what she has known.

LADY M. Here's the smell of the blood still: all the perfumes of Arabia will not sweeten this little hand. Oh, oh, oh!

DOCT. What a sigh is there! The heart is sorely charged.

GENT. I would not have such a heart in my bosom for the dignity[2] of the whole body.

DOCT. Well, well, well,—

GENT. Pray God it be, sir.

DOCT. This disease is beyond my practice:[3] yet I have known those which have walked in their sleep who have died holily in their beds.

LADY M. Wash your hands; put on your nightgown; look not so pale: I tell you yet again, Banquo's buried; he cannot come out on's grave.

DOCT. Even so?

LADY M. To bed, to bed; there's knocking at the gate: come, come, come, come, give me your hand: what's done cannot be undone: to bed, to bed, to bed. [*Exit.*

DOCT. Will she go now to bed?

GENT. Directly.

[2] *dignity*] worth.
[3] *practice*] art, skill.

DOCT. Foul whisperings are abroad: unnatural deeds
Do breed unnatural troubles: infected minds
To their deaf pillows will discharge their secrets:
More needs she the divine than the physician.
God, God forgive us all! Look after her;
Remove from her the means of all annoyance,[4]
And still keep eyes upon her. So good night:
My mind she has mated[5] and amazed my sight:
I think, but dare not speak.

GENT. Good night, good doctor. [*Exeunt*.

SCENE II. *The country near Dunsinane.*

Drum and colours. Enter MENTEITH, CAITHNESS, ANGUS, LENNOX, *and* Soldiers.

MENT. The English power is near, led on by Malcolm,
His uncle Siward and the good Macduff:
Revenges burn in them; for their dear causes
Would to the bleeding and the grim alarm
Excite the mortified man.

ANG. Near Birnam wood
Shall we well meet them; that way are they coming.

CAITH. Who knows if Donalbain be with his brother?

LEN. For certain, sir, he is not: I have a file[1]
Of all the gentry: there is Siward's son,
And many unrough[2] youths, that even now
Protest[3] their first of manhood.

MENT. What does the tyrant?

[4] *annoyance*] injury.
[5] *mated*] confounded.

---

[1] *file*] list.
[2] *unrough*] unbearded.
[3] *protest*] proclaim.

CAITH. Great Dunsinane he strongly fortifies:
Some say he's mad; others, that lesser hate him,
Do call it valiant fury: but, for certain,
He cannot buckle his distemper'd cause
Within the belt of rule.

ANG. Now does he feel
His secret murders sticking on his hands;
Now minutely[4] revolts upbraid his faith-breach;
Those he commands move only in command,
Nothing in love: now does he feel his title
Hang loose about him, like a giant's robe
Upon a dwarfish thief.

MENT. Who then shall blame
His pester'd senses to recoil and start,
When all that is within him does condemn
Itself for being there?

CAITH. Well, march we on,
To give obedience where 'tis truly owed:
Meet we the medicine of the sickly weal,
And with him pour we, in our country's purge,
Each drop of us.

LEN. Or so much as it needs
To dew the sovereign flower and drown the weeds.
Make we our march towards Birnam. [*Exeunt, marching.*

SCENE III. *Dunsinane. A room in the castle.*

Enter MACBETH, Doctor, *and* Attendants.

MACB. Bring me no more reports; let them fly all:
Till Birnam wood remove to Dunsinane
I cannot taint[1] with fear. What's the boy Malcolm?
Was he not born of woman? The spirits that know
All mortal consequences have pronounced me thus:

[4] *minutely*] continual.

[1] *taint*] be infected.

'Fear not, Macbeth; no man that's born of woman
Shall e'er have power upon thee.' Then fly, false thanes,
And mingle with the English epicures:
The mind I sway[2] by and the heart I bear
Shall never sag with doubt nor shake with fear.

Enter a Servant.

The devil damn thee black, thou cream-faced loon![3]
Where got'st thou that goose look?

SERV. There is ten thousand—

MACB. Geese, villain?

SERV. Soldiers, sir.

MACB. Go prick thy face and over-red thy fear,
Thou lily-liver'd boy. What soldiers, patch?[4]
Death of thy soul! those linen cheeks of thine
Are counsellors to fear. What soldiers, whey-face?

SERV. The English force, so please you.

MACB. Take thy face hence. [*Exit Servant*.
Seyton!—I am sick at heart,
When I behold—Seyton, I say!—This push[5]
Will cheer me ever, or disseat me now.
I have lived long enough: my way[6] of life
Is fall'n into the sear, the yellow leaf,
And that which should accompany old age,
As honour, love, obedience, troops of friends,
I must not look to have; but, in their stead,
Curses, not loud but deep, mouth-honour, breath,
Which the poor heart would fain deny, and dare not.
Seyton!

Enter SEYTON.

SEY. What's your gracious pleasure?

[2] *sway*] rule myself.
[3] *loon*] brute, rogue.
[4] *patch*] clown, fool.
[5] *push*] attack.
[6] *way*] course, term.

MACB. What news more?
SEY. All is confirm'd, my lord, which was reported.
MACB. I'll fight, till from my bones my flesh be hack'd.
Give me my armour.
SEY. 'Tis not needed yet.
MACB. I'll put it on.
Send out moe[7] horses, skirr[8] the country round;
Hang those that talk of fear. Give me mine armour.
How does your patient, doctor?
DOCT. Not so sick, my lord,
As she is troubled with thick-coming fancies,
That keep her from her rest.
MACB. Cure her of that.
Canst thou not minister to a mind diseased,
Pluck from the memory a rooted sorrow,
Raze out the written troubles of the brain,
And with some sweet oblivious antidote
Cleanse the stuff'd bosom of that perilous stuff
Which weighs upon the heart?
DOCT. Therein the patient
Must minister to himself.
MACB. Throw physic to the dogs, I'll none of it.
Come, put mine armour on; give me my staff.
Seyton, send out. Doctor, the thanes fly from me.
Come, sir, dispatch. If thou couldst, doctor, cast
The water[9] of my land, find her disease
And purge it to a sound and pristine health,
I would applaud thee to the very echo,
That should applaud again. Pull't off, I say.
What rhubarb, senna,[10] or what purgative drug,
Would scour these English hence? Hear'st thou of them?
DOCT. Ay, my good lord; your royal preparation
Makes us hear something.
MACB. Bring it[11] after me.

[7] *moe*] more.
[8] *skirr*] move rapidly, scour.
[9] *cast The water*] inspect the urine.
[10] *senna*] Cassia senna, a plant used as a purgative.
[11] *it*] i.e., a piece of Macbeth's armor.

I will not be afraid of death and bane
Till Birnam forest come to Dunsinane.

DOCT. [*Aside*] Were I from Dunsinane away and clear,
Profit again should hardly draw me here. [*Exeunt.*

SCENE IV. *Country near Birnam wood.*

Drum and colours. Enter MALCOLM, *old* SIWARD *and his* Son, MACDUFF, MENTEITH, CAITHNESS, ANGUS, LENNOX, ROSS, *and* Soldiers, *marching.*

MAL. Cousins, I hope the days are near at hand
That chambers will be safe.

MENT. We doubt it nothing.

SIW. What wood is this before us?

MENT. The wood of Birnam.

MAL. Let every soldier hew him down a bough,
And bear't before him: thereby shall we shadow
The numbers of our host, and make discovery
Err in report of us.

SOLDIERS. It shall be done.

SIW. We learn no other but the confident tyrant
Keeps still in Dunsinane, and will endure
Our setting down before't.

MAL. 'Tis his main hope:
For where there is advantage[1] to be given,
Both more and less have given him the revolt,
And none serve with him but constrained things
Whose hearts are absent too.

MACD. Let our just censures
Attend the true event, and put we on
Industrious soldiership.

[1] *advantage*] opportunity.

SIW. The time approaches,
That will with due decision make us know
What we shall say we have and what we owe.
Thoughts speculative their unsure hopes relate,
But certain issue strokes must arbitrate:
Towards which advance the war. [*Exeunt, marching.*

SCENE V. *Dunsinane. Within the castle.*

Enter MACBETH, SEYTON, *and* Soldiers, *with drum and colours.*

MACB. Hang out our banners on the outward walls;
The cry is still 'They come': our castle's strength
Will laugh a siege to scorn: here let them lie
Till famine and the ague eat them up:
Were they not forced[1] with those that should be ours,
We might have met them dareful,[2] beard to beard,
And beat them backward home. [*A cry of women within.*
What is that noise?

SEY. It is the cry of women, my good lord. [*Exit.*

MACB. I have almost forgot the taste of fears:
The time has been, my senses would have cool'd
To hear a night-shriek, and my fell of hair[3]
Would at a dismal treatise[4] rouse and stir
As life were in't: I have supp'd full with horrors;
Direness,[5] familiar to my slaughterous thoughts,
Cannot once start me.

Re-enter SEYTON.

Wherefore was that cry?

SEY. The queen, my lord, is dead.

[1] *forced*] reinforced.
[2] *dareful*] boldly.
[3] *fell of hair*] hairy skin.
[4] *treatise*] tale.
[5] *Direness*] horror.

MACB. She should have died hereafter;
There would have been a time for such a word.
To-morrow, and to-morrow, and to-morrow,
Creeps in this petty pace from day to day,
To the last syllable of recorded time;
And all our yesterdays have lighted fools
The way to dusty death. Out, out, brief candle!
Life's but a walking shadow, a poor player
That struts and frets his hour upon the stage
And then is heard no more: it is a tale
Told by an idiot, full of sound and fury,
Signifying nothing.

Enter a MESSENGER.

Thou comest to use thy tongue; thy story quickly.
MESS. Gracious my lord,
I should report that which I say I saw,
But know not how to do it.
MACB. Well, say, sir.
MESS. As I did stand my watch upon the hill,
I look'd toward Birnam, and anon, methought,
The wood began to move.
MACB. Liar and slave!
MESS. Let me endure your wrath, if't be not so:
Within this three mile may you see it coming;
I say, a moving grove.
MACB. If thou speak'st false,
Upon the next tree shalt thou hang alive,
Till famine cling[6] thee: if thy speech be sooth,
I care not if thou dost for me as much.
I pull in resolution, and begin
To doubt the equivocation of the fiend
That lies like truth: 'Fear not, till Birnam wood
Do come to Dunsinane'; and now a wood
Comes toward Dunsinane. Arm, arm, and out!
If this which he avouches does appear,
There is nor flying hence nor tarrying here.
I 'gin to be a-weary of the sun,

[6] *cling*] shrivel.

And wish the estate o' the world were now undone.
Ring the alarum-bell! Blow, wind! come, wrack!
At least we'll die with harness on our back. [*Exeunt.*

SCENE VI. *Dunsinane. Before the castle.*

Drum and colours. Enter MALCOLM, *old* SIWARD, MACDUFF, *and their* Army, *with boughs.*

MAL. Now near enough; your leavy screens throw down,
And show like those you are. You, worthy uncle,
Shall, with my cousin, your right noble son,
Lead our first battle:[1] worthy Macduff and we
Shall take upon's what else remains to do,
According to our order.

SIW. Fare you well.
Do we but find the tyrant's power to-night,
Let us be beaten, if we cannot fight.

MACD. Make all our trumpets speak; give them all breath,
Those clamorous harbingers of blood and death. [*Exeunt.*

SCENE VII. *Another part of the field.*

Alarums. Enter MACBETH.

MACB. They have tied me to a stake; I cannot fly,
But bear-like I must fight the course. What's he
That was not born of woman? Such a one
Am I to fear, or none.

Enter young SIWARD.

[1] *battle*] army.

YO. SIW. What is thy name?
MACB. Thou'lt be afraid to hear it.
YO. SIW. No; though thou call'st thyself a hotter name
Than any is in hell.
MACB. My name's Macbeth.
YO. SIW. The devil himself could not pronounce a title
More hateful to mine ear.
MACB. No, nor more fearful.
YO. SIW. Thou liest, abhorred tyrant; with my sword
I'll prove the lie thou speak'st.
[*They fight, and young Siward is slain.*
MACB. Thou wast born of woman.
But swords I smile at, weapons laugh to scorn,
Brandish'd by man that's of a woman born. [*Exit.*

Alarums. Enter MACDUFF.

MACD. That way the noise is. Tyrant, show thy face!
If thou be'st slain and with no stroke of mine,
My wife and children's ghosts will haunt me still.
I cannot strike at wretched kerns,[1] whose arms
Are hired to bear their staves:[2] either thou, Macbeth,
Or else my sword, with an unbatter'd edge,
I sheathe again undeeded. There thou shouldst be;
By this great clatter, one of greatest note
Seems bruited:[3] let me find him, fortune!
And more I beg not. [*Exit. Alarums.*

Enter MALCOLM *and old* SIWARD.

SIW. This way, my lord; the castle's gently render'd:[4]
The tyrant's people on both sides do fight;
The noble thanes do bravely in the war;
The day almost itself professes yours,
And little is to do.
MAL. We have met with foes

[1] *kerns*] Irish mercenaries.
[2] *staves*] spear shafts.
[3] *bruited*] reported.
[4] *gently render'd*] surrendered unreluctantly.

That strike beside us.

SIW. Enter, sir, the castle. [*Exeunt. Alarum.*

SCENE VIII. *Another part of the field.*

Enter MACBETH.

MACB. Why should I play the Roman fool, and die
On mine own sword? whiles I see lives, the gashes
Do better upon them.

Enter MACDUFF.

MACD. Turn, hell-hound, turn!

MACB. Of all men else I have avoided thee:
But get thee back; my soul is too much charged
With blood of thine already.

MACD. I have no words:
My voice is in my sword, thou bloodier villain
Than terms can give thee out! [*They fight.*

MACB. Thou losest labour:
As easy mayst thou the intrenchant[1] air
With thy keen sword impress as make me bleed:
Let fall thy blade on vulnerable crests;
I bear a charmed life, which must not yield
To one of woman born.

MACD. Despair thy charm,
And let the angel whom thou still hast served
Tell thee, Macduff was from his mother's womb
Untimely ripp'd.

MACB. Accursed be that tongue that tells me so,
For it hath cow'd my better part of man!
And be these juggling fiends no more believed,
That palter[2] with us in a double sense;
That keep the word of promise to our ear,

[1] *intrenchant*] invulnerable.
[2] *palter*] shuffle, equivocate.

And break it to our hope. I'll not fight with thee.

MACD. Then yield thee, coward,
And live to be the show and gaze o' the time:
We'll have thee, as our rarer monsters are,
Painted upon a pole, and underwrit,
'Here may you see the tyrant.'

MACB. I will not yield,
To kiss the ground before young Malcolm's feet,
And to be baited with the rabble's curse.
Though Birnam wood be come to Dunsinane,
And thou opposed, being of no woman born,
Yet I will try the last: before my body
I throw my warlike shield: lay on, Macduff;
And damn'd be him that first cries 'Hold, enough!'
[*Exeunt, fighting. Alarums.*

Retreat. Flourish. Enter, with drum and colours, MALCOLM, *old* SIWARD, ROSS, *the other* Thanes, *and* Soldiers.

MAL. I would the friends we miss were safe arrived.

SIW. Some must go off: and yet, by these I see,
So great a day as this is cheaply bought.

MAL. Macduff is missing, and your noble son.

ROSS. Your son, my lord, has paid a soldier's debt:
He only lived but till he was a man;
The which no sooner had his prowess confirm'd
In the unshrinking station where he fought,
But like a man he died.

SIW. Then he is dead?

ROSS. Ay, and brought off the field: your cause of sorrow
Must not be measured by his worth, for then
It hath no end.

SIW. Had he his hurts before?

ROSS. Ay, on the front.

SIW. Why then, God's soldier be he!
Had I as many sons as I have hairs,
I would not wish them to a fairer death:
And so his knell is knoll'd.

MAL. He's worth more sorrow,
And that I'll spend for him.

SIW. He's worth no more:
They say he parted well and paid his score:
And so God be with him! Here comes newer comfort.

Re-enter MACDUFF, *with* MACBETH'S *head*.

MACD. Hail, king! for so thou art: behold, where stands
The usurper's cursed head: the time is free:
I see thee compass'd with thy kingdom's pearl,
That speak my salutation in their minds;
Whose voices I desire aloud with mine:
Hail, King of Scotland!

ALL. Hail, King of Scotland! [*Flourish*.

MAL. We shall not spend a large expense of time
Before we reckon with your several loves,
And make us even with you. My thanes and kinsmen,
Henceforth be earls, the first that ever Scotland
In such an honour named. What's more to do,
Which would be planted newly with the time,
As calling home our exiled friends abroad
That fled the snares of watchful tyranny,
Producing forth the cruel ministers
Of this dead butcher and his fiend-like queen,
Who, as 'tis thought, by self and violent hands
Took off her life; this, and what needful else
That calls upon us, by the grace of Grace
We will perform in measure, time and place:
So thanks to all at once and to each one,
Whom we invite to see us crown'd at Scone.
[*Flourish. Exeunt*.

PLAYS

THE MIKADO, William Schwenck Gilbert. 64pp. 27268-0
FAUST, PART ONE, Johann Wolfgang von Goethe. 192pp. 28046-2
THE INSPECTOR GENERAL, Nikolai Gogol. 80pp. 28500-6
SHE STOOPS TO CONQUER, Oliver Goldsmith. 80pp. 26867-5
A DOLL'S HOUSE, Henrik Ibsen. 80pp. 27062-9
GHOSTS, Henrik Ibsen. 64pp. 29852-3
HEDDA GABLER, Henrik Ibsen. 80pp. 26469-6
THE WILD DUCK, Henrik Ibsen. 96pp. 41116-8
VOLPONE, Ben Jonson. 112pp. 28049-7
DR. FAUSTUS, Christopher Marlowe. 64pp. 28208-2
THE MISANTHROPE, Molière. 64pp. 27065-3
ANNA CHRISTIE, Eugene O'Neill. 80pp. 29985-6
BEYOND THE HORIZON, Eugene O'Neill. 96pp. 29085-9
THE EMPEROR JONES, Eugene O'Neill. 64pp. 29268-1
THE LONG VOYAGE HOME AND OTHER PLAYS, Eugene O'Neill. 80pp. 28755-6
RIGHT YOU ARE, IF YOU THINK YOU ARE, Luigi Pirandello. 64pp. (Not available in Europe or United Kingdom.) 29576-1
SIX CHARACTERS IN SEARCH OF AN AUTHOR, Luigi Pirandello. 64pp. (Not available in Europe or United Kingdom.) 29992-9
PHÈDRE, Jean Racine. 64pp. 41927-4
HANDS AROUND, Arthur Schnitzler. 64pp. 28724-6
ANTONY AND CLEOPATRA, William Shakespeare. 128pp. 40062-X
AS YOU LIKE IT, William Shakespeare. 80pp. 40432-3
HAMLET, William Shakespeare. 128pp. 27278-8
HENRY IV, William Shakespeare. 96pp. 29584-2
JULIUS CAESAR, William Shakespeare. 80pp. 26876-4
KING LEAR, William Shakespeare. 112pp. 28058-6
LOVE'S LABOUR'S LOST, William Shakespeare. 64pp. 41929-0
MACBETH, William Shakespeare. 96pp. 27802-6
MEASURE FOR MEASURE, William Shakespeare. 96pp. 40889-2
THE MERCHANT OF VENICE, William Shakespeare. 96pp. 28492-1
A MIDSUMMER NIGHT'S DREAM, William Shakespeare. 80pp. 27067-X
MUCH ADO ABOUT NOTHING, William Shakespeare. 80pp. 28272-4
OTHELLO, William Shakespeare. 112pp. 29097-2
RICHARD III, William Shakespeare. 112pp. 28747-5
ROMEO AND JULIET, William Shakespeare. 96pp. 27557-4
THE TAMING OF THE SHREW, William Shakespeare. 96pp. 29765-9
THE TEMPEST, William Shakespeare. 96pp. 40658-X
TWELFTH NIGHT; OR, WHAT YOU WILL, William Shakespeare. 80pp. 29290-8
ARMS AND THE MAN, George Bernard Shaw. 80pp. (Not available in Europe or United Kingdom.) 26476-9
HEARTBREAK HOUSE, George Bernard Shaw. 128pp. (Not available in Europe or United Kingdom.) 29291-6
PYGMALION; George Bernard Shaw. 96pp. (Available in U.S. only.) 28222-8
THE RIVALS, Richard Brinsley Sheridan. 96pp. 40433-1
THE SCHOOL FOR SCANDAL, Richard Brinsley Sheridan. 96pp. 26687-7
ANTIGONE, Sophocles. 64pp. 27804-2
OEDIPUS AT COLONUS, Sophocles. 64pp. 40659-8
OEDIPUS REX, Sophocles. 64pp. 26877-2